01195

Razor Eyes

RAZOR EYES

by Richard Hough

LODESTAR BOOKS

E. P. Dutton   New York

First published in the U.S.A. 1983 by E. P. Dutton
2 Park Avenue, New York, N.Y. 10016

First published in Great Britain 1981 by J.M. Dent & Sons Limited,
Aldine House, 33 Welbeck Street, London W1M 8LX

Library of Congress Cataloging in Publication Data

Hough, Richard Alexander, date
   Razor Eyes.

   "Lodestar books."
   Summary: More than forty years after the fact, a
farmer details his experiences as a British pilot in
World War II and the maturing effect they had on him.
   1. World War, 1939–1945—England—Juvenile fiction.
[1. World War, 1939–1945—England—Fiction. 2. Great
Britain—History—20th century—Fiction] I. Title.
PZ7.H8142Raz 1983 [Fic] 83-11574
ISBN 0-525-66916-7

Printed in the U.S.A. OBE
10 9 8 7 6 5 4 3 2

for Aidan Chambers with gratitude

Contents

CHAPTER ONE

The Perfect Three-Pointer

I picked up the big, cold, rusting revolver, a Smith and Wesson .38, standard issue. Nothing very special about it. Of course, it was illegal to possess it without a license. But I could truly plead ignorance. I had no idea I still had it.

I picked it out of the old box and held it snug in my right hand, and it was as if I had thrown a switch—a switch marked "memory"—and the current at once began to flow in full flood. Those three shots I had fired all those years ago had signaled, in a way, the end of my boyhood, the beginning of my manhood. And signaled, too, the end of Bruno.

Then I broke open the big, cold, rusting revolver and stared, now in near disbelief, at the three chambers still loaded with live rounds, the other three chambers with empty cases. I had never reloaded after firing the gun all those years ago, and then screaming "Ambulance—for God's sake send the ambulance!"

My name is Mick Boyd, retired farmer, and I am writing about some of the things that happened to me between the ages of eighteen and twenty-three. I am doing this because the other day I was moving, after forty-one years. The mess! I had to clear the potting shed, the coal hole, half a barn, the cupboard under the stairs, the attic. In the attic, as well as the Smith and Wesson, was a pair of cracked old goggles, and a cardboard box which fell to pieces when I picked it up.

Papers everywhere. Some of them were held together by paper clips, rusted now with age and leaving their brown imprint when removed. One letter was from my mother, dated June 12, 1942.

Dear Mick,
How are things going? Well, I'm sure. You'll survive. . . .

I was averaging around three ops a week at the time, and I mean flying operations against the enemy, not operations under the surgeon's knife, which would have been safer. Typical of Mum, that throw-away optimism.

Then I spotted some more once familiar handwriting. It was Bruno's. Like him, it was elegant, even stately, the ink now brown with age. So was the paper it was written on: R.A.F. Station, Helmsley Green, West Sussex. Dated July 27, 1942.

Dear Razor [that was my nickname then],
There is a truly wizard W.A.A.F. here, Brenda, very dark soft hair. I'm nuts about her. Had a dodgy "do" yesterday, a Wing show. Charlie Best and old 'arry 'awkins in B Flight bought it, and at 13,000 feet my flight commander had to jump, and brolley hopped down near Amiens. Served him right.
Charlie was saying the other day—"Imagine being old!" He had had a few jars, but I know what he meant. I mean, I wouldn't mind surviving this lot, settling down with some bird. But who wants to live till about 1980 and get all wrinkled . . . ?

The date when I found the revolver, and read Bruno's letter, was August 27, 1983, forty-one years later. I had lived till 1983, and I had got a bit wrinkled, but I was very glad to be alive. So would Bruno have been, I'm sure. But he "bought it" a month after he wrote that letter, back in '42.

I picked up the scattered letters. As soon as I was settled into our new house, with plenty of time to spare, I decided to write all this down just as if I were writing to Bruno, in the language we all used years ago—as a memorial to him, if you like, and to remind me how lucky young Razor had been.

I was born and brought up in the south London suburb of Croydon. My father was a senior clerk in a large insurance company in Croydon. He would sometimes say, "If times were better, I would get out of this rut and on to the land—run a small farm, something like that." Of course he never did. I loved him dearly, but fate had decreed the unspectacular life for him.

He served in World War I but remained a clerk—"A khaki clerk," he would remark self-mockingly as he carefully filled his pipe—and he never heard a shot fired in anger.

My mother died only recently. As an old woman, she remained beautiful in a handsome sort of way. I still have her wedding photograph, taken in 1917, my father a corporal, with a mustache, a shy expression on his face, unable to believe his luck, wearing puttees and belt blancoed stunning white.

My mother was only an inch taller than my father but her high, elaborate hat with its veil settled on to her piled-up mass of red hair makes the difference appear greater in this photograph. I imagine their honeymoon was a mixture of shyness, happiness, and wonder, with a restlessness overcoming my mother as the days passed and there was no work, nothing for her busy hands to do.

She was a very positive woman, a good mother who did not fuss or fret and just got on with things, not by any means in

silence. She could have handled a family of ten children without trouble, instead of just Jo and me. I am not sure why there
were only the two of us. I seem to recall many years ago
hushed talk about there being some danger if she had another
child. It seemed to me indelicate to raise the matter again.

So it was just the four of us in a modest-sized, detached
house with a garden mainly of roses, which my mother loved,
a grass tennis court, and a garage for the car, which had a name
—Jessica—in the fashion of the 1930s. "Come on, old girl!" my
father would urge on the car on long steep hills, leaning forward against the steering wheel.

One typical exchange will serve to show my relationship
with my sister Jo. She was only a year older than me but at
sixteen she was a good deal stronger, and bolder.

It was on a summer holiday in the Lake District mountains.
We were on Striding Edge, that knifelike ridge extending
from near the summit of Helvellyn. It was bitterly cold and the
four of us were huddled in the lee of a rock eating our sand-
wiches. I was feeling uneasy about the loose scree that fell away
evermore steeply below us.

We were ready to leave, and I stood up to help my mother
with her rucksack. I clumsily let go of a strap and the rucksack
fell, at once gathering speed down the loose rocks until it was
held by a single boulder.

"I'll fetch it," I said, my stomach turning at the prospect, one
hand resting on my mother's shoulder. "I'll go."

I could feel Jo's eyes on me. Her timing was perfect. Just
when I really thought I could do it—oh yes, surely I could,
taking it step by step—she called out, "Oh fooey!" and ran
through scree down the fifty feet, sliding to a halt beside the
rock, throwing the rucksack over her shoulder, and bringing
it back.

"You didn't need to do that. I was just going." But I was so
ashamed and so furious that I found it hard to say the words.

"That's all right—no risk."

I was fifteen at the time, but I almost cried myself to sleep that night in the old farmhouse where we stayed. "No risk!"

Looking back, I think now that Jo was probably provoked into doing things like that by my own reluctance to take risks, or perhaps she thought she could brace me up by her own example. Like our mother, she was a great bracer. You can pass your own judgment on Jo when I write more about her later. At that time I was half fearful of her, half admiring, and certainly proud of her in front of my friends even if she did sometimes discomfort me.

The trouble with Jo was that, as my sister, she knew me too well, especially my weaknesses. She liked to show off her fearlessness in front of me because she knew I was easily scared —not scared especially of heights, or even of death, but of being hurt. I could not bear hurt or injury to any person, animal, or above all to myself. Always, as a boy, I was afraid of anything that might lead to blood and pain. Even someone else's cut finger would make me feel sick. And a recurrent nightmare featured lacerated flesh, broken bones, innards torn asunder.

I was ashamed of being so weak—but there you are, I was born with this fear, and Jo knew it.

The high point of those school years were the holidays in the Lake District. We always stayed in farmhouses, very cheaply, walking and climbing all day regardless of the weather, which in August is often terrible. We got soaked through most days. The one time it did not rain was when we climbed up through the cloud like a plane and came out into the clear sun and a world of dazzling white, broken only by the granite tips of the highest mountain peaks stretching away in all directions.

It was on one of those days that I first discovered that I had exceptional eyesight. I was about twelve at the time, conscious that I was mediocre in almost every department, and certainly not bold in spirit, and the discovery gave me immense satisfaction. From the summit of Great Gable where I was standing with my father and Jo, the billowy clouds drifted around us. The island next to ours in this white ocean was Kirk Fell, nearly a mile away. And there, lying in a crevice, was a figure. I could see it quite clearly, with a bundle—probably a rucksack —a few feet below.

"Oh rubbish!" exclaimed Jo characteristically, dismissing the possibility at once when I pointed out the figure.

My father looked more carefully, following my directions. He had good eyes and never wore glasses, but he could not see it. "I think you're imagining it, son. We'll find out if anyone's missing when we get down, but we don't want to waste the time of the rescue parties."

He was wrong and I was right. A young man foolish enough to climb on his own in dodgy weather, was missing, and the rescuers found him in the nick of time and in the exact position I had described. Jo said that I had not pointed out the right spot to her. But nothing could dilute my pleasure, and I am sure I boasted about my eyes to my friends.

There is a lot of talk today about the threat of nuclear war destroying civilization and wiping life off the face of the earth. It is difficult for people who were not alive at the time to understand that my generation, too, grew up in the threatening likelihood of cities being flattened and life extinguished by bombs and chemical and gas warfare. And during the late 1930s, every month seemed to bring world war nearer as Germany, Japan, and Italy threatened and invaded smaller and weaker nations and the arms race grew faster and faster. The truth is that every generation thinks that it is unique and the one singled out by the fates to be the last on earth.

My parents had lived through the 1914–1918 "war to end wars" as it was hopefully called. By 1938, when I was sixteen, it seemed certain that another world war must soon break out. Every day new signs of it appeared in the newspapers, and at the cinema the newsreels were full of pictures of the civil war in Spain and the fighting in China. At school we helped to dig air-raid shelters, tearing up the flower beds outside the classrooms, filling sandbags and piling them around the windows.

We were all issued rubber gas masks with transparent fronts that misted up. We had gas parade once a week when we all lined up in the quad and practiced putting our gas masks on quickly. Bruno got the hang of making the most terrible rude noise by blowing out very hard. We all made this noise in chorus one day and the Head came out of his study in a paroxysm of fury. "You don't seem to understand that this is a matter of life and death, but you all deserve to die anyway —twisting in agony from gas poisoning."

When he disappeared the whole school squirmed and twisted in agony and collapsed and pretended to die, making the terrible rude noise.

Bruno was my best friend at North Court Grammar School. He was taller than me and very thin. "I have a *willowy* figure," he would say self-mockingly. "Just plain skinny," I'd say. He had an olive complexion and never had a spot on his chin, just soft down. There was a dignity about him, too. And that was certainly something I did not have. The girls loved him and he had one passionate affair after another, even then. He took his love affairs very seriously. I used to try to take the steam out of them by teasing him as I did not think it was good for him to get so involved when we had exams looming.

Our fanatical interest was planes. Airplanes were almost as important as girls in Bruno's life, and I once saw him lose a girl because of one. He was flirting with her at the corner of Melbury Road outside the school when the morning Hannibal from Paris roared overhead at 200 feet. Bruno followed it with his eyes as it lost height, leveled off, held just above the ground, and touched down.

"A perfect three-pointer!" Bruno sighed admiringly. He was always talking about perfect three-pointers. It was either,

"Look at that, Mick, a perfect three-pointer" or "*Not* a perfect three-pointer."

On this occasion, all Bruno's admiration for the Hannibal pilot lost him what admiration he might have enjoyed from his girl, because she got fed up waiting for his attention and made a perfect take-off on her bike in the opposite direction. And that was that.

I remember laughing until the tears poured down my cheeks but Bruno did not think it funny at all—not until later.

I do not know whether we should have been so mad about planes if we had not both lived close to Croydon Aerodrome, in my case our garden flanking the perimeter. With a pair of binoculars plus my marvelous eyesight I could check on the identity of every machine and watch the entire sequence of takeoff and landing. There were memorable "first" days—the day when the first of the new Fokkers flew in from Frankfurt, the day when I spotted the largest and most beautiful machine I had ever seen, Imperial Airways' first De Havilland Albatross, slowly circling like the beautiful bird after which it was named, and then lowering its undercarriage for the final approach while my hands shook with excitement.

Bruno was at my house for tea on the greatest day of all, in the autumn of 1938. We heard them first. We were used to engine noise right overhead when the wind was from the south, but this was like no noise either of us had heard before, and it shook the house and threatened to bring down the ceiling.

We were doing our homework, and now we dropped everything and raced out through the French windows on to the lawn. The planes were so low that we did not see them at once, and then they appeared from the direction of Kenley, three of them, almost grazing the chimney pots, in perfect steady V formation.

I picked them out first, dark against the dark hillside and from photographs recognized them at once. A few seconds later, Bruno spotted them. "My God—Hurricanes!" His exclamation was almost an incantation.

They were the first we had seen of this revolutionary 300 mph fighter. Retractable undercarriage, enclosed cockpit, eight machine guns, 1,000 hp Rolls-Royce engine—this beautiful monoplane made all the R.A.F.'s earlier fighters seem like something put together by the Wright brothers.

I grabbed my binoculars from their hook by the door and watched the planes lower their undercarriages in unison. "They're coming in."

Bruno put out a hand. "Let's have a look." At the end of their downwind leg, I saw them lower their flaps, and with canopies slid back now, bank and turn through 180 degrees for the final approach and touchdown.

Three perfect three-pointers for Bruno to admire! Then the Hurricanes taxied fast away from the watch tower instead of towards it, and were swallowed up inside a hangar on the far side of the field like shy animals anxious to conceal themselves. But that night I went to sleep with a warm feeling of pride and comfort at their proximity. The Germans could boast about their mighty Luftwaffe, but we had the best fighters in the world to shoot down any bombers they might send in time of war.

The next day I started on a model of a Hurricane in my garden workshop to add to my collection.

CHAPTER TWO

One-One-Os with Bombs

It is very important to explain as clearly as possible what I felt at this time, and what others like Bruno felt, as far as I could judge. As I have already written, we were constantly being reminded of the likelihood of war. By early 1939 it seemed impossible that it would not come. We were a year older and would soon be old enough to serve king and country; or, put another way, were ripe for cannon fodder.

When we talked about this at all, it was mockingly and in terms more of cannon fodder than patriotic service. When we should have been earnestly discussing our careers, by 1939 we talked only of what service and what branch we should join. Most of the boys were going to try for the army, because their fathers had served in the army during World War I. Not a Guards regiment or the 4th Hussars, or anything like that. Croydon being in Surrey, most of them thought of a Surrey regiment, and some of them were already cadets or in the Territorial Army—the Terriers.

Quite a number—"Beefy" Bradwell and the Saunders twins among them—were determined to go to sea, again because their fathers had served in the Grand Fleet. Surprisingly few wanted to fly. Bruno's and my enthusiasm made up for the lack of numbers. We were the "I.B.s"—the Intrepid Birdmen—filling our notebooks with drawings of Blenheim and Battle light bombers, great twin-engined Heyfords, and fighters like Gauntlets and Gladiators, and of course the sleek, swift Hurricane.

But even at that time, aged seventeen, a fight within me had already broken out, months before the real world war began. Others had a struggle, too. There were boys at school from pacifist homes who talked about their consciences and how it was wrong to kill. They were not going to fight at all. They were going to join the Peace Pledge Union, or the Quaker Friends Ambulance Unit. They got roundly condemned as cowards, though not by Bruno or me. Theirs was a difficult struggle, but at least they had the courage to let the world watch it.

My trouble was strictly private. One romantic half of me longed above all else in the world to be in the cockpit of a fighter (surely never a Hurricane?—that would be too wonderful to believe!) diving down out of the sun on an enemy formation of bombers, guns blazing. I could see this self-portrait quite clearly and with pleasure: silk scarf, top button undone, helmet and goggles, parachute and harness over my shoulders.

But the satisfaction was not complete for one important reason. The picture itself was not complete, either. There were features that clashed. There was, for instance, the frozen agony of fear, like a dagger-sharp icicle plunged into my body, that struck me when my practical mind told me that streams of return fire would be aimed back at me, that an enemy fighter on my tail could fill my machine with bullets and I felt the agony of one tearing into my hip, another through my chest, soaking my Sidcot suit with blood: my nightmare become reality.

Well, so why didn't I talk about this to Bruno, and maybe other friends, too? Why did I take it so damn seriously? I talked about everything else with Bruno, especially anything about planes and flying—why not this important question? It is difficult to say, even after all the years that have passed. Was it a young man's pride? Fear of being thought a fool or a coward, or different from everyone else? Shame?

The answer, I am sure now, was fear of showing fear, as it had been on Striding Edge and on countless other occasions when faced with the test of courage. No one else at school or among my friends talked about fear. I was sure they never felt it, either. Not this terrible fear of being hurt. I was a freak, I was diseased. That's what I told myself. I had loudly and frequently claimed that I was going to be a fighter pilot. I had never spoken of the terror that the prospect aroused. War was inevitably coming, and I would inevitably be involved. That was what concerned me above everything else during the spring and summer months of 1939 that ended in the explosion of late August when war came at last.

On September 3, Bruno and his parents called on us after morning church. I liked Bruno's mother and father. They were a cheerful couple, easygoing, his father rather lazy I always thought but probably nicer for that, though not at all well off. They often came on Sundays for a few glasses of beer and a chat. Sometimes they stayed for lunch, too. This time they had come to hear a broadcast on the radio. The Prime Minister was delivering a message to the nation, and it was to be so important that everyone felt the need for the comfort of numbers, just as people in the past formed themselves naturally into groups when threatened by an enemy.

We knew what the Prime Minister was going to say, but when he spoke the words "and consequently this country is at war with Germany," I felt that icy shaft entering my body again, and that sickness in my stomach.

For a moment it was as if no one else existed, that *I* was the only enemy, that Germany, which had so far never been thwarted, had marched into country after country, was now hell-bent on *my* destruction, was after *my* blood.

We all went out on to the lawn after the broadcast, thank goodness, for I felt as if I was suffocating indoors. My father and Bruno's pa began fooling about and horseplaying in a grotesque effort to cheer everyone up. No one seemed to know for sure how to behave or what to do in these unique circumstances.

Our world was suddenly at war, and full of clichés like "a nightmare has become reality." And yet nothing had changed. The canary in its cage next door, which was put out on warm days, was singing away. There was the distant murmur of traffic on the Brighton road, my mother was bringing out a tray of glasses. Bruno and I looked at each other, and for once he had nothing to say. What did one say under these circumstances? Only clichés. "Well, now this is it at last!"

Then, thanks be to God, the air-raid sirens began groaning into action. One over towards Kenley first, then another, then the nearest one, on the police station down Beauchamp Road, like an old tenor a bit past his prime trying to discover the right note and finding he had turned into a soprano, and then a screamer, and finally a moaner. Up and down, up and down, caterwauling away.

I suppose most of England was paralyzed during the next seconds, paralyzed in expectation of the worst. As before, I could think only of myself, and of the freezing shaft of fear that was sinking deeper and deeper. . . . So it had come.

Jo never believed in hanging around. The war had started, and the very next day she went into Croydon and joined the W.A.A.F.s. In two weeks she was in her uniform, looking very smart and not in the least self-conscious, as though she had just bought a new dress. She was above average in height, like our mother, and I thought she looked marvelous, in spite of having most of her hair cut off, and said so.

"You can have a uniform, too, if you want it," she said tartly.

I knew what she meant at once, even if there had not been that familiar provocative note in her voice. All over the country there were recruiting posters. The one for the R.A.F. showed a pilot in full flying gear looking up at the sky. VOLUNTEERS FOR FLYING DUTIES it read in large letters. And then, below, You can be accepted NOW for the R.A.F. as a Pilot.

The condition was that you had to be at least eighteen. "I'm too young," I said. "Until September."

"You can put your age up—they'll never know," she said. She never bothered to argue, our Jo.

I could never look the R.A.F. poster straight in the eye after that. I had an uncle who put his age up in World War I. He was fifteen, and he was still only seventeen with a gallantry medal before the army found out, and that was only because he had a Mauser bullet through his head. I told myself that my parents would have a fit if I lied about my age, and then felt guilty because I was not sure they might not have been proud if I had.

I never told Bruno about this. He was eighteen in August, and we had both decided a long time ago that we would be at the recruiting office on our birthdays. It had become a sort of compulsion as far as I was concerned, like waiting half in terror for the sports day finals, only a hundred times more so, the days marching on implacably.

As always, Bruno and I talked a lot about flying and planes and the air war, and like a couple of naturalists drooling over an undiscovered new species, we studied a photograph in the newspapers of the first German plane to be shot down. It was a Heinkel III, riddled with a Hurricane's bullets.

Some of the older senior boys went off to the army that winter, but there were no air raids, and not much fighting. It was "the phony war" and no one seemed to take it very seriously. The only casualties were in the blackout when people walked into lampposts and one another and—occasionally— cars. Rationing of food started but it was not very serious. My father put the car up on to blocks "for the duration." The worst thing about that first winter of war was the cold.

In the early spring of 1940, coming off the soccer field with Bruno and a few others, I remember Bruno saying, "This stupid war's going to fizzle out before we have a chance of having a go."

Jimmy Hanwell, the worst swearer in the school said, "Oh bloody hell, Bruno. You wait."

To my shame, I remember a lifting of my spirits, as though relieved of a great burden, at Bruno's words, and a new equally sudden sinking of them again at Jimmy's outburst.

Over the next weeks we read of air battles over Norway, of Hurricanes and Gladiators fighting Messerschmitts, of Royal Navy dive bombers sinking a German cruiser, and then of the German invasion of Holland and Belgium and France. Instead of hanging out our washing on the Siegfried Line, the Germans overran France in a few weeks, and it was all the British army could do to escape back across the Channel, without their weapons, from Dunkirk.

Two events of that summer of 1940 stand out in my memory. One was just after Dunkirk, in June, and at home we had been listening to the news on the radio. My mother was knitting, as usual when there was nothing else to do with her hands, and my father sighed and leaned forward in his chair to reach his pipe and tobacco pouch in his pocket. "Well, I can see no hope for us now. The whole of Europe conquered and not an ally in sight. They'll just march in."

My mother did not look up from her knitting as she said firmly, "Rubbish, dear. They'll have to swim the Channel first."

I have no doubt that the discussion continued, but I left them, saying I had some homework. I lay on my bed, looking out across Croydon Aerodrome in the summer evening light. It was surrounded by coils of barbed wire now and guarded by sentries. There was a Lewis gun a hundred yards away, set on a stand in a dugout and pointing to the sky. The hangars had all been camouflage-painted.

All civil planes had long since left, and all we saw regularly were Hurricanes of a fighter squadron, whose movements were frequent and furtive. As I watched now, a flight of six of them took off in a long line abreast across the grass, tails lifting, then wheels bouncing several times before clearing the ground and at once tucking up into the wings, right wheel always a fraction ahead of the left wheel, as they climbed towards the setting sun.

Half an hour later, I heard the distant sounds of their Merlin engines again. When I opened the window and looked out, I could see them high above the London balloons that floated like silver toy pigs over the city to "catch" enemy planes. It was already twilight down here, but for the Hurricane pilots it was still blazing daylight, and as they banked towards Croydon again in line, the sun picked up and reflected on their windshields in turn with a brief sparkle like a signal, "Here we come!"

That was one more moment when my love and longing for flying seized me, and the danger element was as distant and harmless as the setting sun.

The second occasion was in August. Much had happened in the weeks between. Both my mother and my father had been proved half right. The chance of winning the war against the massive strength of Germany, and Italy too now, seemed as hopeless as ever. But the German army had not been able to march in. Nor could it cross the Channel without destroying the British navy and air force first.

The main struggle was in the skies above us, where the R.A.F. fighters fought against the overwhelmingly powerful Luftwaffe for the survival of Britain. It was the first battle for a nation that everyone could watch, and on those long summer days the sounds were of wailing sirens, dying away to be replaced by the faint *whoomph-whoomph-whoomph* of distant antiaircraft guns, the rise and fall in volume of aircraft engines, and—faint and intermittent and awesome in its message—the riffle of machine-gun fire 20,000 feet and more above.

Sometimes we could see, far to the south, the pattern of white vapor trails etched swiftly by invisible machines against the blue dome of the sky, tracing the shape of desperate violence and fading again almost instantly. Even at the great height at which the battles were usually fought, there would be sudden diamondlike reflections from wing or windshield, the tiny glow of an explosion followed by a vertical trail of smoke.

One day Bruno and I were at cricket practice, and half a dozen of our friends were around on the playing field—which was always available to us during school holidays—when we heard the distant roar of aircraft engines. For most of that day we had been aware of battle sound like a deep-throated murmur of conversation, rising and falling. This was different—more immediate, closer, the volume rising rapidly.

I was the first to spot them, as usual, but it was someone else who shouted, "Crikey, look at *that!*"

"Bloody hell!" shouted Hanwell.

"They're One-One-Os," I called out. Unmistakable. I had modeled one only the other day. Twin fins, twin engines, distinguishable from the Dornier bomber by its long cockpit canopy set far back. Bruno halted in the middle of his bowling run and stared towards the east, where a tight pack of Messerschmitt 110s, fifteen in all, were power-diving over the Downs, clearly hell-bent for Croydon itself.

They were traveling at a higher speed than any aircraft we had ever seen—impossible to catch, was my first reaction.

Someone was going to try. While we watched the German

machines on their last deadly approach, some of us already spread-eagled on the grass, there came a sudden explosion of even greater sound. Immediately above us—only a hundred feet or so—nine Hurricanes screamed overhead, blue-gray smoke streaming from their engine exhaust stubs, undercarriages already slotted home into the wing undersides.

A great air battle was about to break out, and we were in what Hanwell would have called "the bloody middle, mate."

When the bombs started to go off—*whoomph, whoomph*!— I saw one throw off the roof of a hangar and send up a cloud of smoke and fragments twice as high as those Hurricanes had been flying. Then, like everyone else, I put my head down and tried to pretend that I had buried myself and could not be hurt. The raid lasted about two minutes, the noise lasted much longer. A lot of bombs were delayed action, the *crrrump* sending out blast waves that hit you like a slap in the face, and the sound of the strafing machine guns and cannon continued and faded into the distance as the dogfights between Hurricanes and Messerschmitts worked across Surrey and Sussex.

During a lull I heard Bruno calling out, "Come on, let's go and see." He was on his bicycle and was pedaling away like mad towards the main road that goes past the east side of the airfield. I would have preferred to go home, but I forced myself to follow him.

Black smoke was rising from the watch tower and the terminal building, hangars and small factories on the perimeter. An ammunition store must have been hit, too, and the intermittent cracks and deeper explosions killed the other sounds of catastrophe—the shouts and distant screams and whistles, and the ringing of ambulance and fire-engine bells.

There were police and wardens all over the place, trying to stop the traffic and people like us from getting through. But we slipped past, without any trouble, Bruno and I alone now, and raced as far as we dared go on the road, leaned our bikes against the high fencing, and by standing on our seat saddles, we could see the full extent of the devastation. And pretty terrible it was, too.

Then, as a mocking postscript, and as proof of what surprise had been achieved by the German raiders, the air-raid sirens began wailing out all over Croydon.

"Better bloody late than bloody never." It was, inevitably, Hanwell, who had caught up with us and was leaning over the fence a few yards further down.

Another voice, deeper and angry with fright, shouted, "Get off there—get home, you boys." It was an R.A.F. officer, tin hat pushed back above his blackened face, his uniform filthy. "There are D.A.s all over the place."

I suppose he meant delayed action bombs. But before we had time to jump down we all turned and looked up as a shadow passed over us. The fact that it made only a whistling sound, that it was more like a ghost of a Hurricane, added to the horror of what followed. White vapor streamed from under the dead engine, the tail was almost shot off, the torn fabric revealing the wooden skeleton like a man's ribs, and the machine was yawing from side to side.

The pilot had his hood open, and I could see him quite clearly, his goggles up over his helmet, the fur collar of his Irvine jacket, even the cable to his earphones. He was alive, trying to control the almost uncontrollable, but both his life and control of his Hurricane were to end together split seconds later. The dive was far too steep, his elevator controls had gone. And two hundred yards in front of us—Hanwell and Bruno, the R.A.F. officer with the blackened face, and maybe a dozen more people near the spot—the maimed Hurricane hit the grass, sending up a cloud of dust and earth, cartwheeled once on wings that folded and crumpled to nothing, was catapulted up twenty feet into the air and fell back to explode like another Messerschmitt's bomb.

Blue and yellow flames. Smoke that was at first gray then oily black spiraling up high. Crackle and flash of exploding ammunition. Another gush of flame, a merciful one this time, that seemed to tidy up the wreckage, and leave little more than charred, smoking fragments about a crater that held what might have been an engine, pieces of undercarriage and— though I saw nothing—the incinerated remains of a pilot.

Oh yes, I was cocky when I got back home, where the French windows had blown in and my mother was crying and sweeping up the glass and fragments of one of her best vases. Cocky as anything. "I saw the whole thing." And, "Gosh, Mum, you should have seen . . ." But I realized quite soon that this was not right and that she was sick with worry about me and my father, who was out too. So I helped her clear up, and it was while I was emptying some more bits of glass into the trash can that I saw that my hands were shaking.

I did not dare take the cup of tea my mother offered me and my father when he came home at last. I could not have held it steadily, and I could not have drunk it because I was feeling too sick.

So I went upstairs to my room. The windows had been smashed there, too. I lay on my bed and sobbed for that pilot, and his poor mutilated, burned body. I felt the fear breaking over me like waves when you're lying on the shore and there is nothing you can do to stop them, except to get up and run. And I couldn't do that, either.

It was eight o'clock and the sun was low. The murmur of catastrophe still spread out from the airfield, bringing with it the pungent smell of burning and death which I was to come to know so well. I remembered that it was Bruno's birthday in two days' time, and mine in three weeks. I was committed, and there was no escape. The thought of the expression on Bruno's face, the icy contempt of Jo, the mockery of the boys at school —these were an even worse prospect than the march of events I had laid down for myself. My birthday would come as night follows day, and as death followed life for that Hurricane pilot.

CHAPTER THREE

The Big Decision

The flight lieutenant did not even look up from his desk when I handed over my completed form. "Right, the corporal in the next office will give you your railway warrant and instructions for your medical."

No one said, "Well, that's very good of you. Just the sort of fellow we want." After all, I was telling myself, I am a volunteer. I don't *have* to offer to lay down my life for my country.

From the moment I had entered the recruiting station, I had been treated as a number, just as I was later given a number like some criminal—1338428 Aircraftsman Second Class Boyd, M. Then it was the long journey to Weston-super-Mare for the medical. They were very strict, I had been told. Bruno had sailed through his. "Nothing to it," he had said. But (and I could hardly admit it even to myself) there was a small flame of hope burning inside me that I would fail, that there would be some hidden weakness that would prevent me from qualifying as a pilot.

The medical took nearly all day, and the only comment I got was from the eye man who watched me read off the bottom line with both left and right eye as if it had been a newspaper headline. "The first one today who's been able to do that," he said.

The only human touch was provided by the final interviewing officer, who asked abruptly, "Do you think you'll be any good as a pilot?"

I said that I hoped that I would. Then he looked at me in silence for several seconds, and I thought, "He does this all the time and he's so practiced that he can see the truth. Even now he knows that I've got this character disability—he knows that when it comes to the first moment of danger, I shall reveal it. He can tell every shade of courage from blind recklessness to blue funk . . ."

All he said was "What made you think of the air force?"

And I explained about living beside Croydon Aerodrome and making models and reading about planes with Bruno. "He joined up three weeks ago," I said.

After that, he became quite human and shook my hand and told me my papers would be coming through shortly. In the train on the way back to London, I eyed my fellow passengers —the elderly woman who wanted the window open in spite of the smoke and soot, the father and son who never spoke, and the rest, and I thought, "You'll be looking at me differently soon—in my uniform, with wings, perhaps my top button undone to show I'm a fighter pilot."

And at once I felt ashamed. "Bloody cocky and a bloody coward!" as Jimmy Hanwell would say if he knew. But he never would know. No one would ever know, thank God. And the feeling of buoyancy I had experienced as I left that interviewing officer's room collapsed. Life was going to be difficult enough without having to conceal so much.

When I got home, my father asked how it had gone. When I told him, he said, "I can't pretend I'm not afraid for you, son. It wouldn't be true to say that. But it is true that I feel very proud and know that you'll do your best. I didn't get near the fighting in the last lot, and it left me with a bit of a scar." Then he quoted that bit of Johnson, "Every man thinks meanly of himself for not having been a soldier . . ."

He was always so straight, my father, and as I felt like throwing my arms around his neck at that moment, I also experienced a sense of shame that, by contrast, I seemed to have so many mean doubts. Where could I have got them from? Not from my mother, either, who at that moment pushed the door open with her knee and marched in with an enormous tray of tea.

"Well, Mick—they didn't find anything wrong with you, I know. Always been fit as a fiddle, like me. When do you start flying?" If she felt any anxiety, she was not going to show it. Not Mum.

"A touch of left rudder. That's it. Now center the stick. Now take off hands and feet. See? She's stable. Flying herself."

The voice came through the Gosport tube in gentle, coaxing tones. Flight Lieutenant Osborne was a dedicated, patient instructor, who really persuaded you that you were almost ready to go solo from the first flip.

It was a rare, clear November day in 1940. The daylight air battles of the summer were over. As the nights had grown longer in October, the Germans had stopped coming over in daylight. R.A.F. Fighter Command had not broken, the invasion had never been launched, and the Battle of Britain (as it was now called) was won.

Now the German bombers came over at night, switching their attacks to the nation's cities. All the prewar fears of total destruction seemed as if they were being realized. Only the other night, the heart of Coventry had been smashed and burned down.

"Now ninety degrees to port. Stick and rudder together. Keep her nose up. Right."

In the patchwork of Cambridgeshire fields, some arable

green, others rich brown from the plough, the training airfield was not much larger than these, its identity marked by the hangars on the east side, the compound of domestic huts, messes, stores, and parade ground behind. Two Tiger Moths were taking off from the grass in formation, their shadows forming at once, then diminishing in size and clarity as they climbed. The windsock in the southwest corner was pointing south.

"Right—I'll take over." I felt the authority of the touch on rudder pedals and joystick. "The wind's not as strong as I thought. So what do we do to lose height quickly?"

My instructor turned sharply to port again on to the final approach. I knew that he had made no mistake and that he only wanted to show me a maneuver.

"We sideslip in—like this." The nose of the Moth went up, I felt the left rudder being pushed hard, and at the same time the stick was pushed firmly to its extremity to the right.

The little biplane skidded through the air at an acute angle, dropping at an alarming speed. At about 200 feet, Osborne straightened her out and leveled her off to a modest glide angle just as if he had put out a hand and plucked the plane out of the air.

"You'll find this useful sometimes, but you'll have to watch it with a Hurricane—they drop like stones. Now let's see you put her down."

It was the first time and I felt a sudden breath of panic. But the patient voice steadied me, and I knew that he could take over the controls in an instant.

"That's it—back—back. Glance down at the A.S.I. You should be doing about forty for this final glide. Hold her there. No, don't touch the rudder. Just let her stall . . . and sit."

It was not clean, not what Bruno would call "a perfect three-pointer," but there had been worse first landings. She bounced three or four feet; my instructor resisted what must have been a strong temptation to take over with his set of controls. And the Tiger Moth was on the ground.

"Now taxi her clear, there's another coming in. A few more like that and you'll be able to solo."

And so I did, a few days later, in foul conditions, with a light drizzle falling and cloud base at 1,500 feet, what we called "Harry Clampers." "I wouldn't send everyone up for the first time in this, but you'll be all right," said Osborne matter-of-factly. Goodness, what a lot I owed that flight lieutenant, for filling me with a self-confidence I had never before known, as well as his patient and meticulous instruction!

On December 3, 1940, I opened up the throttle of my little Tiger Moth and went bumping across the grass with an empty cockpit between me and the 130 hp Gypsy Major engine, and at about 35 mph pulled back gently on the stick. I was airborne. And I was alone. More alone than I had ever been, but with an exquisite sense of freedom I had never experienced before. To anyone who has not done it, I would liken it to driving a fast motor bicycle three-dimensionally, with no obstruction except the earth itself far below.

From the time I had had my uniform thrown at me by a foul-mouthed corporal in the clothing store, through those early weeks of ground training—marching, stripping Lewis guns, elementary school on Tiger Moths, to advanced training—there had been scarcely a moment to think, let alone brood on my fears.

Adolescent introspection began to fade simply because I was so busy and so preoccupied with mastering this new skill of flying. Nightmares disappeared for the same reason: I was so dead tired when I got to bed, I went out like the barrack-room light at 10:30. All that I knew during these weeks was that I was being swept along willy-nilly and helplessly, as if on some tidal race. I was vaguely conscious of being reshaped on the R.A.F. production line, aware that any sort of boasting was sat on very sharply as "shooting a line," that discipline for air crew was slacker than for ground crew, but all the same, you called officers "sir" and stood to attention when you talked to them, and that any lack of enthusiasm to get at the enemy and volunteer for any dangerous work around, was called "yellow."

There must have been a sort of pause in this headlong rush of training—an intermission—briefly when, on arrival at an Operational Training Unit in Scotland, I faced a Hurricane for the first time as a pilot. It was a memorable, reverential moment.

"She's more lovely than I dreamt!" I remember exclaiming naively to my instructor.

"Never mind her fancy looks, it's what you do to her that matters," he said coarsely. He was, unlike Flight Lieutenant Osborne, a hardened regular who had been shot down twice in the Battle of Britain and been sent, resenting it, to Training Command for a rest.

But his unaesthetic attitude could not spoil the wonder of the Hurricane's reality. It was like a film fan meeting his favorite star face to face, it was like being offered the hand and a smile of your current soccer hero. Remembering the magic moment when Bruno and I had seen that section of Hurricanes circling Croydon for the first time, I wished now that he was here to share this experience, instead of being somewhere in Canada completing his training.

"All right, young sprog, get in and learn the controls."

I hoisted myself on to the port wing of the monoplane, and climbed over the sill into the compact cockpit, facing the blind flying panel, an array of more instrument dials, the reflector gun sight, the spade gripstick with its gun button and brake lever, and the assorted controls—flaps and undercarriage, seat adjustment, and other levers on each side.

"Now for the cockpit drill before take off." In a tone close to exasperation at the boredom of it all, my new instructor worked through the ground drill. Ten minutes later he was standing on the tarmac under the wingtip, hands in pocket, staring at me morosely as I went through the drill for the last time. Then I called out to the ground crew, "Contact!" The

Merlin burst into life, and the three-bladed Rotol airscrew was a blur through the bulletproof, heavily slanted windshield.

The casualties at this O.T.U. were appalling. Three or four times a month, we would be detailed in turn to funeral parties for u / t (under training) pilots' deaths. The weather on this west coast of Scotland in winter was dreadful and we could only fly on perhaps one day in three. Pilots got lost in the cloud and murk—I did, twice—and flew into the sea or the nearest mountain. It seemed an insane place to have a training station, but we just flew on there, and like the casualty rate in World War I on the Western Front, or in the Battle of Britain, the longer you survived, the better you got and the better your chances of survival. It was as simple as that.

The low standard of instructors did not help. It was pitiful to see a new group arrive, full of eagerness to learn, and then to hear at the bar only a week or two later the tone of defiance or disillusion in their voices. And, too often, "Here's to poor old Taffy—he bought it today."

My instructor turned out to be the rough brute I had suspected him to be from the first. At least we did not share the machine and he could not snatch the controls from my hands as he must often have wanted to do. But he would fly beside me in his Hurricane and order me to take off in formation, and tuck my wings in close to his in the air. No matter how great the turbulence, he would curse at me over the R / T if I did not stay glued to him. Then it would be mock dogfights, and he could bounce me out of the sun, or shout at me, "Come on, you terrible sprog!" as I struggled to hold his tail, giving short bursts with the camera gun—which would later show that I had not hit him once.

But there were also flights of ecstasy, especially on rare clear moonlight nights, when I was alone and the R / T was silent, and I knew that I had mastered this sweetly responsive little fighter. It was like a dance together in perfect harmony and freedom as I looped and slow-rolled her at 20,000 feet, and then dived steeply towards the glittering sea, leveling off at 100 feet and rocking my wings in celebration.

At the same time, I knew that this was not the real world. The real world in the spring of 1941 was the small island of Britain separated by twenty-three miles from the great hostile land mass of Europe, where the war machines of Germany and Italy had overrun almost the whole continent. What chance did we have against these hundreds of millions? The newspapers made brave headlines of our bomber offensive against Germany, but everyone in the R.A.F. knew how puny this was and how savage our losses. How could we ever win the war against these odds?

Once or twice a week, Fighter Command bulletins were distributed, typewritten duplicated reports on offensive operations. "Kenley and Biggin Hill Wings—Offensive Sweep—St. Omer—Missing, Sergeant W. Boston, Sergeant M. Mostyn 217 Squadron, Pilot Officers Fredericks and Mason 609 Squadron, wounded, Flight Lieutenant W. Weston 111 Squadron. 2 Messerschmitt 109s believed damaged."

Now that we were fighting over enemy territory and on the offensive, and so many of our best pilots had been killed in the Battle of Britain, our losses almost always appeared greater than those of the Germans.

Every time I read one of those bulletins, my imagination would screen images of combat like a camera gun—no longer distant pictures seen as a schoolboy from the ground at Croydon, but as immediate close-ups with the tracer fire screaming into the machine alongside me, the cry, "Break—break, for Christ's sake," the machine now only a ball of falling fire trailing a stream of oil-black smoke.

"Sergeant M. Mostyn, missing . . ." Missing because there was nothing left of him. I would remember that word "missing" when I was flying. And suddenly there would be the simulated rattle of machine guns over the R / T, my instructor would sweep past within yards above me, calling out, "That's the third time I've shot you down, Sergeant Boyd," the voice barking with triumph. I had been bounced out of a cloud again. And the old fear of mutilation and pain, which I thought had been driven away, was back like some specter.

In another month, our course at O.T.U. would be over, and we would be assigned to squadrons and be "on ops," an expression with a brave, hard ring to it. But as far as I was concerned (though a million pounds would not have been enough to get me to confess it) it also sent a chill through me and brought before my eyes for the thousandth time the picture of that Hurricane exploding at Croydon back in those innocent days when I was still at school.

On the last evening before passing out of O.T.U., half a dozen on my course went down to the pub in the nearest village. It was a traditional time to celebrate, and some cheerful W.A.A.F.s came with us. On the way there, we linked arms and sang in discordant chorus "Roll out the Barrel" and "She'll be coming round the mountain," and there was a lot of giggling and necking even before we arrived.

I especially missed Bruno on these occasions. I had made a few friends on the course among the other sergeants—I had not applied for a commission at that time, and was content with three stripes on my sleeve and the informality of the sergeants' mess. But I had not yet met anyone I could talk to about anything except shop and W.A.A.F.s and our instructors.

I had learned to put down a few pints of beer by now without making a fool of myself, and that evening we drank quite a lot, sang quite a lot, and played a lot of rather bad darts. Halfway through the evening, I went out into the dark for a breath of air. A fellow called Chris Wallace came with me. He was from north London somewhere, a year older than me, and had had a rough time with his instructor, too. I did not know him very well, but the beer had loosened our tongues, and he suddenly said to me, "I don't know about you, Mick, but I'm going to volunteer for Training Command next week."

"How's that?" I asked. One or two of each course were often sent to become instructors, a breed that was despised because of the relative safety of the job.

"Well," Wallace explained glibly, with a belch, "I think I would make a good instructor and be more useful for the R.A.F. that way. No one else seems to want to do it, but I don't mind."

"Why not?" I asked myself. In the last weeks, I had been thinking again about the art of teaching flying, and how fascinated I had been experiencing Osborne's skill at E.F.T.S., and horrified at how bad and wasteful it could be at O.T.U. with poor instructors. I was really beginning to convince myself that I had a vocation for instructing, and that this new interest had no bearing on my old and deep-rooted fears.

As an instructor I would enjoy all the status of being an R.A.F. pilot but without the risks of being in action against the enemy. I did not spell it out to myself in these simple terms at the time, but that was what my subconscious was telling me.

I would be a good instructor. It was my duty to be an instructor. That was what I was saying to myself. Now here was a fellow pilot brave enough to volunteer for instructing, and risk the taunts. It would be easier for both of us if there were two. . . .

Now, to my own amazement but with a deep sense of relief, I found myself saying, "Yes, I rather agree. I'll put my name down if you will."

CHAPTER FOUR

Jo and Vivienne

Midsummer 1941. Bruno was back from Canada and, like me, had finished his O.T.U. By chance, we both got leave at the same time, and who should turn up on the first evening but Jo, an officer in the W.A.A.F. now, looking very smart and pleased with life. Our mother swept into action, relishing the challenge of organizing our entertainment and finding the food from now meager rations for all of us.

Jo had brought a friend with her, a New Zealand girl called Vivienne Macmillan, dark, with a sweet smile, who wanted to help my mother and was always told to go and enjoy herself with us. Luckily, Bruno did not fall for her, because he always got the girls he wanted, more so than ever now that he was a pilot officer with his wings up and a mustache, which made him look very manly and led me to tease him a great deal.

I say it was lucky because, for the first time and after only a couple of days with her, I felt I might—just might—be getting rather fond of her. We talked together for hours, about New Zealand and her life there, and her parents, and the beauty of the country and what life would be like here and in

New Zealand after the war—if we ever won it. She was very easy to talk to, and I think she really was interested when I talked to her about flying.

My father had dug up the tennis court to grow vegetables so we played doubles down on the public courts, and sat outside the Devonshire Arms in the sun and drank pints of beer. Jo and Vivienne were both in R.D.F. (called radar later, after the Americans came into the war) and could not talk much about their work, even to us, and certainly not outside pubs. But they talked about mess life, gossiped about their fellow W.A.A.F.s, and Bruno told us about a visit he had made to New York on a 72-hour leave pass from Canada—"My God, the *food*—steaks that big!"

"Which group do you hope to get into?" Bruno asked me at one point. A signal would arrive at home, I had been told, to tell me the station I was to report to.

"None, really," I said, trying to keep a note of defiance out of my voice. "I'm taking an instructor's course."

"A *what?*" Trust Jo to chip in like that.

There was a very brief moment of silence. I sipped my beer. Bruno said in a normal voice, "You'd make a very good instructor. Not everyone could do it, but I should think you've got the patience."

Vivienne, who knew all about it already, said, "I think it's a wizard idea. It's the most important job of all."

"Just for a bit, anyway. I'll probably get bored with it, then I'll join you on ops," I said to Bruno.

"Spit Vs—that's what I want," he said. "Let's have another pint."

Later, after lunch, when my mother was in the kitchen and Bruno and Vivienne in the garden, Jo and I cleared the table. She reached for the fruit bowl. There was a popular song at the time that everyone was singing, called "An apple for the teacher," and that's what she sang, in a distinctly mocking voice as she threw me one, and then turned on her heel and walked out—very tall and cool in her beautifully tailored officer's uniform.

I took a defiant bite at it. But it was a cooking apple from the garden, and bitter as all hell.

I lived with seven other noncommissioned pilots in a Nissen hut down a muddy road, nearly a mile from the mess. Some joker had scrawled on the wall, "This is the end beyond the end!" It took nearly fifteen minutes to bicycle to a meal or a pint of beer, less time when the ground was frozen.

If R.A.F. Ecclestone had ever possessed any self-respect as an airfield, it had long since lost it by the time I was posted there late in the summer of 1941. Ecclestone was a sort of factory for training instructors, and the most depressing place I had ever seen. All day long, in foul weather and fair weather, the Tiger Moths, Harvards, and Oxfords made circuits and bumps, or flew off on cross-country navigational exercises. Half the u / t instructors were resentful at having been pulled off an operational squadron and thought the whole thing was demeaning, and the other half were like Chris Wallace and me, bearing an unspoken measure of guilt or a chip on the shoulder.

The veterans were stand-offish or patronizing to us at best, and downright hostile at worst and when tanked up on late evenings. Then ugly words like "yellow" and "scrimshanker" were bandied about. Some of us over-reacted to this sort of thing, and I usually responded sharply, thus not improving my popularity among those who had "got some in," like an aggressive Irishman called O'Malley, a flight sergeant and a regular who had been a fitter before the war and had transferred to the flying branch. The gen was that he had been in 9 Group and had not seen much fighting in the Battle of Britain anyway.

The drinking at night was heavy but not very merry. We were miles away from the war in northeast England. The act of flying, which I had glorified as a boy, had become a daily

routine of rate-two turns and 250 feet per minute climbs on a
steady compass course. From Hurricanes in simulated
dogfights, I was back again in Tiger Moths learning how to
teach others to qualify for Hurricanes.

My idealism had shriveled like an old apple, soft and wrinkled and—like Jo's—too bitter to eat.

The only thing that kept a small bud of pride alive was the
letters from Vivienne. "Of *course* you're doing the right
thing," she had told me on the last day of our leave. "You can
save more lives and do more for the war effort instructing well
than going on ops."

She wrote to me at least once a week, always lovingly and
supportively. "Keep your spirits up—the course'll soon be
over, and then you can get on with your real work."

But I knew that instructing was not my real work, and the
course was over as far as I was concerned a week after I got
her letter.

This is what happened. It was a Saturday night in October.
We had been on duty in the morning but thick mist had
prevented any flying and everyone taking the course got bored
down at the dispersal playing pontoon or *vingt-et-un*. After
lunch we were free and most of us went into the town to the
movies before the pubs opened.

I came back early, had supper in the mess, wrote a few
letters, and then dozed off while reading. The heavy mob
among the veterans in the course, all of them hard drinkers,
came into the mess hoping to catch the bar before it closed.
They were not pleased when they failed, and then caught sight
of me in the far corner.

Three of the five disappeared, the other two came over to
where I was sitting. One of them was O'Malley.

"Look who we've got here," he called out when he was
about ten yards away. "One of our brave English boys in blue."
His Irish accent was very strong and he was swaying notice-
ably. "Ah but he knows all about the smell of a 109's exhaust
up his dainty little English nose."

Then I saw him pick up an empty pint glass on the table beside him and throw it hard at me. "Catch!" It struck the corner of my table, splintered and covered me with flying glass.

"That was a fool thing to do," I said. "You'd better sweep it up."

"Don't you tell me what to do. I could've hit you. I always hit the target. And that's more than you've ever done. I know you—stuck up ol'boyo, Boyd." He was advancing on me, an empty bottle of pale ale in his hand.

I did not like the look of this at all, threw aside my book, and got up to meet him, my eyes on the raised bottle. A yard from me he brought it down in a powerful swing. Contrary to his boast, he was not very accurate and I dodged it easily, and grappled with him. He smelled of beer and sweat and I could feel the roughness of his cheek from not shaving that morning.

He was kicking at my shins, painfully, and anger and fear gripped me. I had done boxing for three years at North Court Grammar, and was even in the finals one year, so I was not bad. But my main advantage was that I was sober. He kicked me in the groin, and that was the end of any restraint on my part. I hit him hard on the left cheek, so hard that pain streaked up my arm, and he fell to the floor. But he was very quick and came up again, holding a chair by the leg as he did so.

Besides the awful smell of him, I remember the noise he made, an animal yell and very terrifying. I caught the chair with my left arm, threw it aside, and went in with the classic left-right. O'Malley was slow to dodge—too slow—and he grunted as he took the blows on his head, and half fell. This was no time for good manners, and I kicked the back of one of his legs. As he fell against a table, sending more glasses crashing, I hit him twice more, and twice again on the head after it struck the floor.

Suddenly I realized that he was out—how much as a result of a dozen pints, or the bang on the back of his head, or my punches, there was no way of telling. We were alone, his companion had fled, and the silence was complete. I stood up, with blood dripping from my right knuckles—dripping into a pool of spilt beer.

I had never seen anything so squalid in all my life as this sergeants' mess, late on a Saturday night: broken glass, spilt beer, tables and chairs on their side, this wretched, drunken Irishman lying at my feet in his filthy, stinking uniform.

I remember saying aloud, half laughing with self-disgust because I was frightened of crying, "You're a disgrace to your uniform, to your wings, to the R.A.F.!" If there had been anyone present, he might have thought I was addressing the wretched O'Malley. I was not. I was addressing myself. I had reached my nadir, and enough was enough.

My schoolboy ideals of patriotism, of flying in defense of my country, of all that that recruiting poster had stood for, had ended in *this*. All because I was gutless.

The next morning I put in a chit, a request for permission for an interview with the adjutant. He passed me on to the C.O., a fierce, bitter, middle-aged man with a cockney accent and an M.C. ribbon from World War I under his wings. He shouted at me and said "hell" four times. The gist of it all was: what are you doing wasting R.A.F. time? Can't you make up your stupid mind? And what makes you know you won't change your mind when you get to a squadron and don't like all the flak and jerries?

"Yes, sir. I do see. I have behaved badly. But I am absolutely certain that ops is the right thing for me."

"That hell of an Irishman provoked you, didn't he, Sergeant Boyd?"

I thought nobody knew, except the doctor who swore he would not mention it to a soul, and declared that O'Malley had it coming to him.

"Not really, sir. He only speeded up my decision. And I think it's the right time for me to prove to myself that I can face up to ops."

For several seconds the C.O. remained speechless, and now

purple-faced, uttered an explosive, "Hell, sergeant. Do you think this war was set up so you could prove something to your sniveling self? For your convenience! So you think you can face up to ops now! Do you think the pilots in the Battle of Britain who saved this country a couple of years ago waited about for the sacred moment, when they felt able to fight the enemy? Like hell they did! They just died by the hundred doing their duty."

He paused for breath, and I listened in shamed horror as he said, "This war is not a drunken brawl with an Irishman. This is a struggle for life and freedom and the only way out is to forget precious personal feelings and private wishes, and bloody well win."

The C.O. uttered a single grunt as an exclamation mark to his speech, and dismissed me. I marched out feeling about six inches tall. But within forty-eight hours I had a rail warrant and a posting to West Cowley in Sussex in my pocket. I left terrible R.A.F. Ecclestone without saying a word to a soul. There was nothing I had to say, and I was scared of what might be said to me, by the ex-ops chaps as well as the green boys like me who had never heard a burst of 20 mm cannon fired at them since they joined up.

Vivienne was at a radar station somewhere in Suffolk. I sent her a telegram from the village post office before catching my train south. There was a twenty-four-hour gap between the time I was due in London and the time I had to report at West Cowley. I had looked up the train schedule from her station and said I would meet the 3:32 P.M. at Liverpool Street. *Please try and make it. Love, Mick,* I ended.

Marvelous. She *made* it! I sat on my kitbag with my feet up on my parachute bag, gas-mask case as a hard cushion for my head, breathing the sulfurous, smoky air of the station, waiting for her late train. I saw her break clear of the crowd, mainly sailors, at the barrier, and run towards me.

She threw herself into my arms, her cheek incredibly soft

against mine, and said, "Oh Mick—Mick, what's happened?" in that New Zealand twang I loved so much.

"How did you do it? But you did it—isn't that wizard?"

She drew back, dark brown eyes looking up at me anxiously. "I got a thirty-six-hour pass. But what's the matter, Mick?"

I told her in the train to Croydon, our luggage piled up on the seats to discourage other passengers. It was early evening, just before blackout time, the sky clear, the balloons at 5,000 feet reflecting the last of the autumn sun. There were lights on in some of the houses, Children's Hour on the radio, men clearing the last of the summer vegetables in the back gardens with bonfires burning. An enormous gap and a mountain of rubble in Clapham High Street, and many houses stripped of their roofs, confirmed how recent the blitz had been, and the antiaircraft gun battery surrounded by barbed wire on the Common showed that London was prepared for more.

I think I must have been rather defiant about my decision, because Vivienne said several times, "It's all *right*—if that's what you want, then fine. So you're going on ops after all."

I know what Jo would have said. She would have said, "What's all the fuss about, Mick. You always make such a fuss. Just get on with it."

But I did not really want to make a fuss at all. I just wanted to be with Vivienne for—what was it?—twenty-one hours now. You could say a lot in that time. She had her hat off and her black hair had fallen almost to her shoulders.

"It's not regulation length. It has to be above your collar."

"Don't cheek me, sergeant. I'm your superior officer." She stretched out a hand and put it against my face. "It's nice being in love with a sergeant. And you needn't salute me if you don't want to."

"I want to do much more than salute you."

The electric train lurched to a stop at East Croydon. I threw the kitbag on to my shoulder, and Vivienne gave me a hand with the parachute bag, which was just as heavy. It was almost dark when we got out of the station and difficult to see if there

was a taxi. But we got an ancient Austin in the end, and went
chugging off up the hill towards our road.

That evening we lay about listening to records quietly long
after my parents went upstairs. Then we kissed goodnight.

Sleep should have been serene. It was nothing of the kind.
Something was nagging away at me. I dreamed I was down at
the dispersal hut at West Cowley, which should have been full
of the noise of pilots and ground crew. But I was alone. The
place was empty, the doors of the lockers where we kept our
gear all wide open, and all empty. There was only the duty
corporal at the telephone table, and he was calling out to me
urgently, "What's the matter? What're you waiting for? Get
going for Christ's sake—*scramble*!"

I ran out of the hut. The sky was clear and empty and silent,
and there was only one machine there, a hundred yards away,
a Hurricane with the cockpit hood slid back, parachute draped
ready on the tail. The airfield was deserted, no one in sight
except Jo. She was laughing, mockingly. "Come on, slow-
coach. Get airborne!"

When I began running, I woke up.

I thought I could talk to Vivienne about anything by now.
No secrets. But all that morning, I could not bring myself to
mention this dream to her.

I managed to cast the memory of it out of my mind by
midmorning. The wind on the North Downs helped. Beyond
the possible hearing of anyone but me, she talked of her work
at the radar station, where she was now a controller in the ops
room, and told me of the rough time Jo was having near Dover
—shelled from Cap Gris Nez, bombed and strafed, working
impossible hours. "I think she's all right so far. But the strain
—it's terrific."

Vivienne was working in 12 Group, thank goodness, where
the pace was hot enough but not as bad as Dover.

"I'll be giving you orders if you ever fly up into 12 Group
from West Cowley," she said.

"We'd better have a code word so I'll know."

"That'll confuse everyone," she said. "I'll just say 'over' twice at the end of the message, then you'll know it's me. 'Over, over,' like that."

"I'll recognize your voice however much static there is."

She laughed. "You're teasing me about my accent. Of course you're right. It's easy to forget I don't speak with the same accent as you—us Kiwis." And she exaggerated her accent so that we both laughed.

I glanced at my watch and calculated we had ten more minutes before we had to retrace our steps. I pulled her down on to the soft grass and held her tightly. I was as certain as I could be of anything that this was the last time we could lie like this alone.

Then she pushed me aside. "Enough of that, sergeant, or I'll have you on a charge." We walked to the bus stop, and then home. There was one hour left.

CHAPTER FIVE

The First Flak

They were Hurricane Mark IIbs, the first I had seen, with four Hispano 20 mm cannon, their barrels projecting like probosci from the leading edge of the wings. The Germans had been packing thicker and thicker armor plate on their bombers, which made shooting them down with machine guns very difficult. With four cannon you could blast anything out of the sky with a single half-second burst.

A section of four Hurricanes in loose "finger" formation banked low over the little railway station where the train had dropped me, and with flaps and wheels down descended on their final approach to West Cowley a mile away.

Pride in these machines and a new pride in myself that I was soon to fly them on ops swept over me like a strong tide. I was in a man's world at last, a hard world of endeavor and heroism. I threw my kitbag on to my shoulder and picked up my brown canvas parachute bag—they weighed nothing at all now—and walked down the wooden steps as the four Hurricanes dropped out of sight. A W.A.A.F. driver was waiting for me in a van. "Morning, handsome," she greeted me chirpily. "You for 140 Squadron?"

I nodded and threw my bags into the back. "How are things?"

She tossed the *Daily Mirror* on to my lap and pressed the starter button. "Better. We got a new cook last week. The other one passed out on officers' mess booze. The Squadron Leader Administration's a devil—but aren't they all." She spoke with world-weary resignation.

"And flying? Many ops?" I asked.

I might have guessed the answer. "Oh, flying. Well, yes, there's always flying. I mean—" She broke off to wave to another W.A.A.F. driving in the opposite direction, who slowed and called out,

"Chris—I put your tea behind the stove—ta-ta."

It was beer not tea in the sergeants' mess, and the atmosphere was unlike any I had known before. A flight sergeant with oil stains all over his tunic—there was even oil on his D.F.M. ribbon—was putting back a pint in two long gulps.

"Somebody's got to do something about that lousy flak at St. Quai," he said, wiping the froth from his mouth with the back of his hand. "I nearly bought it this afternoon."

A small sergeant with an out-of-scale mustache nodded over his pint. "Someone like my flight commander. He's going to commit suicide one day anyway. Brought back half a French forest in his intake this morning. We might as well sacrifice him in a good cause." He turned to me and nodded. "You been posted here?"

"Got in from Ecclestone. They were trying to make me into an instructor, but I wasn't having that." Ah, brave words, I told myself.

"Good show. You'll be replacing Green in A Flight."

"Where's he gone?" I stupidly asked.

"Gone? He's gone for a Burton. Last week. Over St. Quentin on a night rhubarb. Somebody thought they saw him blow up. D'you want a pint?"

West Cowley was a new airfield carved out of Sussex farmland behind Beachy Head in the panic of summer 1940 when the Germans were knocking them out faster than craters could be filled and telephone wires reconnected. It had two tarmac runways. This was just as well as we sometimes had crippled or fuel-hungry bombers making emergency landings, which could go arse over tit (R.A.F. for somersaulting) on wet grass.

I learned that 140 Squadron was engaged in day bomber escort work, mainly over France. The Hurricane had got a more powerful Rolls-Royce engine now, but it was still too slow for the modern generation of German fighters. It partly made up for this inadequacy by its maneuverability and toughness. It could take terrible punishment and still get home. During the right moon periods, and when the weather permitted, our Hurricanes used to prowl around German airfields trying to pick off bombers as they came in to land. We called that intruder work, and night rhubarbs were freelance, freeranging operations destroying targets of opportunity at low level with those lethal cannon.

The C.O. of 140 Squadron was a Canadian from Saskatchewan—Squadron Leader Bob Taylor, a steady, democratic type who was much liked by the nonofficer pilots for his easygoing ways and lack of arrogance.

As I came to know everyone better, I got the impression that Taylor was not exactly hero-worshiped by the officer pilots, who liked a C.O. to be colorful and hard-drinking. Personally, I liked his safe, equable nature. He did not do daft things like losing his temper with enemy flak posts and committing suicide down their barrels like some I came to know, before they were killed. But he flew like a dream, and his shooting was sublime. I once saw him going for a locomotive—a great fat black one belching smoke—at very low level, opening fire at 400 yards, the very first shells tearing into the boiler, in spite of some ferocious flak from the open flat wagon at the rear of the train.

My flight commander was Geoff Eliot, an ex-minor public school type with a very grand accent to match. But there was nothing phony about his prowess as a pilot. He had got a rugby blue at Cambridge before the war, suffering the inevitable broken nose, and had applied the same skills to flying a Hurricane: keen eyes, swift reactions, and a dashing spirit.

I met him down at the Flight dispersal on the morning after my arrival. The place teemed with a constant to-ing and fro-ing of pilots, fitters, riggers, armorers, and radio operators, making a nonsense of that dream of mine.

Eliot called me into his office at the rear of the Nissen hut and looked at my record sheet and asked for my log book. "At ease, Boyd," he said after a minute. He was looking up at me with the brightest, clearest blue eyes I had ever seen.

"Ecclestone," he said. "You poor bastard. So they tried to shove you into Training Command."

I thought I had better get things straight right from the start. "No, sir. Actually, I volunteered."

"That's a dashed funny thing to do. Why didn't you want ops?"

"I thought I'd make a good instructor, sir."

Eliot appeared to dismiss the whole curious business from his mind. Mental torment, inner debates and doubts, and the more enquiring side of the human mind were as distant as the moon from his consideration. He was in the business of leadership, flying, war, and winning.

"Get your gear on and we'll do a sector recce together." He stood up and reached for his helmet with all its attachments, hanging on the wall. He was three inches shorter than me, a wiry, squat figure. I could see him as a nippy fly-half on the rugby field. He was smiling at me. It was as if it hurt him because he did it with only half his mouth.

"Are you any good?" he asked provocatively.

"Yes, hot stuff—sir." Was that me saying that? I could hardly believe my ears. But I had a feeling it was the right thing to have said. "And good eyes."

Eliot grunted, and said in dismissal, "Chiefy'll give you a kite."

A tall, fair pilot officer, who looked about as green as me and was called Andy Mitchell, looked up from an ancient copy of *Esquire* as I put on my Irvine jacket and changed into flying boots. "So you're having your test. What he laughingly calls your sector recce."

"Why 'laughingly'?"

"You'll see. Better strap on your revolver. You never know."

A sector reconnaissance was normally a familiarization flight around the sector in which the airfield was situated. Pride and self-consciousness in about equal measure prohibited me from asking any more.

My hands were not shaking as I zipped up my flying boots. They were new "escape" issue boots designed so that with a quick slash with a knife you could cut off the wool-lined calf top, leaving you with what appeared to be a pair of ordinary walking shoes that would be less likely to arouse suspicion if you were shot down over enemy territory.

No, not shaking. But there was a dryness in my throat as I walked out of the hut with a careful casualness, impelled by the same sense of inevitability I had experienced ever since leaving Ecclestone.

I could not stand still or reverse my tracks now, any more than yesterday I could have called out "Stop this train!" Was this what courage was all about really? Was it a negative business, a mere recognition of the impossibility of halting or reversing the trend of events as you were rushed along?

The blast pen where my Hurricane C-Charlie was parked was only a couple of hundred yards distant. But another crashing truth hit my mind before I reached it, with starter trolley acc already plugged in, fitter and rigger and a couple of other erks standing around. It was this. Unlike me, Flight Lieutenant Eliot was not asking these damn-fool questions as he went out to his kite, and had certainly never asked them in his life. He had his mind on the job in hand, and no introspection. And if

I was going to survive, I had better do the same thing—that's what I was thinking as I nodded to the aircraftsman standing on the Hurricane's port wing, waiting to help me with my straps.

"You want about a quarter throttle on this one, sarge. She's a bit temperamental starting."

But the Hurricane started at the first touch of the button, the trolley acc was unplugged and two men stood by the chock ropes.

Yes, mind on the job. Cockpit drill. Trim, mixture, check pitot head, flaps. Check ailerons, elevators. It had been known for cables to get crossed during a service. . . .

The Merlin ticking over was sweet music after the *putter-putter* of a Tiger Moth. I had been told to use button B channel on the ground, and Eliot's voice came over my headphones, at once crisp and authoritative. "We'll do a nice fancy formation takeoff, and switch to button C when we're airborne."

Eliot raised his right hand in its gauntlet glove, pointing ahead down the runway, and when he dropped it forward, his Hurricane began to roll, and I steadily pushed open the throttle through its quadrant.

A minute or two later we were over base at 2,000 feet. "Open up," he ordered me. "Just remember my tail's your responsibility and we don't want to be jumped. Can happen on this side of the Channel."

I looked behind, to both sides, up and down. The old rules of World War I still applied. "A still head's a dead head." That was why we traditionally wore silk scarves, to reduce the effect of constant neck-chafing a collar would have on your skin.

Looking down, I caught a glimpse of fields scattered with tall posts to discourage invading troop carriers and gliders, camouflaged concrete gun posts, and on the seashore where two summers ago holiday-makers picnicked and swam, there was row upon piled row of coiled barbed wire. The German army was still expected, and only a few months earlier had driven us out of Greece and successfully invaded Crete from the air, as well as driving the Russians far back into their homeland.

Meanwhile, Flight Lieutenant Eliot appeared to be taking the war to the enemy, and me with it. We put our noses down off Seaford, steering due south low over the sea and a hundred yards apart. In my flight commander's judgment, our sector evidently included the English Channel.

The Hurricane felt as responsive as I remembered the machine from O.T.U., so sympathetic and eager that she seemed to be an extension of my own physical responses and will. Eliot turned sharply ninety degrees to starboard without warning and I clamped tightly on to his tail, rising to the challenge, while he jinked and turned again, climbing two or three hundred feet and diving back on to the wavetops. When he steadied on a southerly course again I came up loosely abreast and slightly behind his Hurricane. We were very low now, our props seeming to brush the sea, which swept under us like a slate-colored torrent flecked white.

Eliot had his hood thrown back and was looking across at me. I felt marvelous when he raised his left hand with the thumb up before pressing it briefly over his fixed microphone in his oxygen mask to indicate radio silence. A minute or two later he pointed ahead, and I saw a hazy dark line on the horizon with breaks of white. It was the French coast—enemy coast—and the white was the chalk cliffs of Seine Maritime.

I briefly lost sight of the coast under my starboard wing as Eliot turned ninety degrees to port to fly parallel to it. When we straightened out and I could see it again, more clearly now, undulating with the rise and fall of the land, I felt a renewal of the mixed feeling of drama, excitement, and fear which had struck me a few minutes earlier. So *that* was what the enemy was like—a land teeming with men out to kill you, and with the weapons to do just that. It was like the first minutes of the war, when the sirens had sounded out, and the cold stab of recognition that *I* was a target had swept over me; only this sensation was many times stronger and more real.

I saw the ships clearly, could even count them. One, two, three, four, then a big one, five, six, and a small one nearest to us. Probably a convoy headed for Antwerp from Le Havre, hugging the coast for safety and hoping not to be seen. But I could see them all right.

I waggled my wings to draw Eliot's attention, slid back my hood and pointed towards them. For a few seconds he evidently failed to spot them, and I could imagine his irritation. Then he raised a thumb in acknowledgment.

I judged that we were still three miles from them when the nearest ship, the last in the convoy, seemed to throw out tiny sparks from bow to stern, as if every seaman on board had simultaneously begun to send an urgent morse message by Aldis lamp.

It was nothing so innocent. "Here we go!" said Eliot, breaking radio silence now that we had been spotted, and at the same time jinking and skidding his Hurricane to throw the gunners off target. It did not seem to make any difference. Puffs appeared in the sky all round us, like black paint spots from a violently handled brush, and seemingly as harmless until I recognized the bright yellow hearts of the explosions.

A near miss exactly between us knocked my Hurricane sideways as if it had been kicked, and I heard the sharp crack of the heavy shell burst above the sound of my engine.

"We'll go home now," said Eliot in a matter-of-fact voice, and aileroned sharply to port, jinking more violently. The fire from the flak ship still conformed to our every maneuver, intensifying in a last effort before we were out of range.

In thirty more seconds we were clear, the flak now fast-fading spots, and we gained height at full throttle in order to contact base, while I scanned the sky behind and above for Messerschmitt 109s alerted of our presence by the convoy.

"Hullo Skipjack—hullo Skipjack, this is Reindeer Green

One, Reindeer Green One. Enemy convoy five miles north of Fécamp, proceeding northeast three miles from coast. Over."

Eliot's message was instantly if faintly acknowledged. "Thank you, Reindeer Green Two. Are you O.K.? Over."

"Sure thing, baby," snapped Eliot in a terrible mock American accent.

Ten minutes later the English coast rose up on the horizon. It might have been the French coast, white cliffs and all, and I reflected on the irony that the sight of this strip of gray and white must have the same effect on German pilots as the French coast had had on me half an hour earlier.

After we were down, Eliot taxied fast back to the dispersal, leaving me trailing, and jumped out of the cockpit like a jack-in-the-box. He was talking to the C.O. when I came in, parachute over my shoulder. He nodded when he saw me and I saluted. "Enjoy your baptism? Want to go back to Ecclestone?"

I put as much emphasis as I could on my "No, sir." And then, realizing that this might be misconstrued, added clumsily, "Yes, sir—I mean I enjoyed the baptism." But the two were already talking again.

Half an hour later, as I was heading for the sergeants' mess, I heard the roar of engines, and looked up to see a dozen aircraft heading out over Beachy Head, the single torpedo beneath each fuselage clearly visible.

"Poor devils!" I heard someone say when the sound had faded. "Their chop rate's sky high." And I imagined them going in low, slow and steady on their targets, the flak intensifying every second, the 37 mm and then the 20 mm and finally the machine-gun fire joining in. And if they survived that, the 109s would be on their tail as they came out of the target area.

But they would not, after all, be alone. Just before I went through the door, I saw several people looking north and pointing out two squadrons of high-flying Spitfires in finger-four battle formation—the torpedo bombers' escort.

"There's going to be a hell of a donny over there," an Australian flight sergeant said. "Stiffen the snakes, why the hell didn't they scramble *us*?"

Later in the war I became practiced and quick at recognizing the nature of a squadron and a station. In late October 1941, when I first arrived at West Cowley, I was still slow and green, and bewildered, too. An operational station was new to me, the routine was new, every face was new. It was like being set down as a complete stranger in a small town in which everyone was busy and—when they noticed you at all—expected you to know who everyone was, where everything was, and what you were supposed to do.

The sergeants' mess bar was the place to meet your fellow N.C.O. pilots, and where most of the shop talk took place. And as I was anxious to get to know people and learn what went on and how to do it, I spent a lot of time there drinking beer, listening, and occasionally chipping in.

The sergeant with the outsize mustache was one of the heaviest beer drinkers. He was called Bill Otway and came from Portsmouth. "My father's in the navy, been in it all his life. So was his dad," he told me. "He thought I was mad when I said I wanted to fly, then he said what about the Fleet Air Arm, and so I said, 'Look, Dad, you know better than me that's only for the posh—only officers can be pilots in the navy.' 'I'll make you an officer,' he said. But I wasn't having any of that, so I got out and joined this mob. He didn't speak to me for six months."

I liked Bill. Some of 140 who had got a lot of ops in could not be bothered with a new sprog. But Bill Otway was all right. He had done about forty ops and liked passing on the tips he had picked up. He had very dark brown eyes and an earnest manner when he was talking flying, and there was always white beer froth on his handlebar mustache when he was drinking, which was most of the time in the mess.

"Most types get clobbered because they get too excited," he told me on my second evening at West Cowley. "They open fire at 500 yards thinking they'll never get a jerry in their sights again, *and*—now listen to this if you don't want to go for a Burton in your first scrap: there are three things to check before you open fire. Not just deflection and range." He sank half a jar in one swallow and wiped some of the froth off his mustache. "That's one. The other two you know about but it's a wonder how many people forget. Check turn-and-bank, check tail. Then, and only then, press the button. And don't take more than a fifth of a second checking or you'll have lost your jerry."

The rest of his beer went down, and I said, "Thanks—have another?"

The sergeants' mess was friendly, like a big pub with everyone wearing the same clothes. Usually there was dance music on the radio, or someone put on a Glen Miller record. There was darts and a lot of talk, which got noisier as the evening wore on. Then someone who had been drinking lemonade would leave. "Got a rhubarb at midnight."

"Good luck, Jacko." "You know why he's such a keen type? Got this French bird outside Boulogne and a handy field to put down in. Ten minutes with 'er while the prop ticks over . . ."

CHAPTER SIX

First Blood

November 3. A wet afternoon. A wag down at dispersal said, "Even the gulls won't get airborne—look." And he was right. They just sat there, in a row on a hangar roof. Eliot said to me, "Boyd, I want you for a show at 0700."

I got up, very casual, voice very flat. "Right, sir."

I did not ask what. That was something I had learned. Eliot liked to wait for the briefing. But of course everyone else knew in minutes. Spy was the most talkative Intelligence Officer in 11 Group and loved passing on the gen that did not matter.

'Same old stuff. Escort 5 Group. Probably St. Omer or Ribeville. Hornchurch Spits top cover. It'll be a wing show. But met. says it'll be duff—I mean, just look outside. Harry Clampers. That's November for you."

I realize that that must sound like double-Dutch. But it is how we used to talk. What I knew it to mean, and instantly at the time, was that we would be escorting Blenheim light bombers to a German airfield at dawn. Our Hurricanes would give close defense, while a wing of Spitfires would provide an umbrella above against the inevitable 109s. But the weather forecast was not good.

Well, it's what you came for, isn't it? I remember mentally rebuking myself. It's what you wanted—or you'd still be at Ecclestone on Moths. Just for God's sake appear normal, like everyone else. So there would be a show tomorrow, and I'd be on it, and so would Bill Otway, and Jack Newcombe from Sydney, and Flight Sergeant Woolley, who didn't even look up from his poker game when he heard.

So I lit a cigarette and sauntered hands in pockets to the oil-stained map that had been stuck to the wall weeks ago with four odd nails. I knew where St. Omer was, but Ribeville? There it was, east of Rouen and at least fifty miles inland. Oh well, met. says it'll be duff.

But of course it was not. November 4 was a clear late autumn day, crisp and fresh. Bacon and air-crew eggs (no one else got them—civilians were rationed to two a month) at 0600. I felt much colder than the morning and ate in my Irvine jacket, both hands hugging the mug of sweet tea to warm them and keep the mug steady to my lips.

The van arrived as inevitably as the train that had brought me here, a sleepy W.A.A.F. driver in yards of scarf at the wheel, a cigarette between her lips. She kept her sleepy eyes on the windshield as we clambered into the back. "We are going to a Flight dispersal—OK?" she asked huskily.

Eliot was there, of course, shaved and spruce, as businesslike as a rugby captain before the final, everything worked out, flying boots polished by his batman that morning, I guessed. "Where's Pilot Officer Seagrave? Ah, Michael, you're late. Sit down all of you. . . ."

We might have missed the rendezvous with the Blenheims if I had not spotted them. As I was to learn later, before the days of airborne radar (and it was then only just being fitted to a few night fighters) it was terribly easy to miss a rendez-vous. The sky is a hell of a big place and visibility, even on the best days, is nearly always restricted in northern Europe.

Anyway, no one else seemed to have seen them, twenty-four

tiny dots right in the sun, flying south in Hendon-style formation. I would get into trouble breaking radio silence. Or would
I, if the C.O. had not seen them—nor the flight commanders?
But we were supposed to be close support, and the French
coast was already looming up.

I threw over the switch and transmitted briefly, "Nine
o'clock high—Green Two out."

There was no acknowledgment, and I began to think—"Oh
God, now I'm in for it." Then the C.O. indicated a turn to
port, and we all followed, opening throttle wide to catch up.

The C.O. tucked us in above and slightly behind, throttled
right back so as not to overshoot. It was clear enough to see
both coasts like two pieces of white-edged jigsaw puzzle separated by the strip of water. In peacetime there would be the
wakes of cross-Channel steamers scoring the sea, and mer-
chantmen steaming up and down. Now it was just an empty
blue no-man's-land. In another three minutes' flying, the heav-
ies—the big flak guns—north of St. Pol opened up like staccato
shouts of hate, and the sky about the Blenheims was at once
stained with white puffs. They were going for us, too, and we
spread out, dropping and gaining height irregularly and sometimes violently.

It was easier for us than for the Blenheims, with their full
bomb loads and lack of nippiness, and most of the flak was
concentrating on them.

The first one went suddenly and mercifully. A direct hit
from a heavy shell caused the last of the bombers to disin-
tegrate. My eyes were directly on it when it exploded. There
was a blue-and-white flash, a blast of black smoke turning gray,
and then there was nothing—no Blenheim, no engines, no
crew, no bombs even. Just a rapidly dissolving puff of smoke
and black specks in the clear sky that might have been fragments of a plane floating down to earth. Or they might have
been . . . ?

The sudden image of those torn-asunder bodies flashed

through my mind like a forgotten nightmare suddenly re-
called. I fought against the old enemy, knowing that if fear
won now it could claim my life. "No introspection!" I
screamed at myself silently. "No squeamish nonsense! They're
dead, that's all. Dead. And you'll be dead, too, if you don't pay
attention. No one else is taking any notice."

Certainly no one spoke on the R / T. Not a word. No "Poor
old Watson, that's his lot!," no "Christ, tough tit for them!"
The next words over the air were, "Five degrees port, Reindeer. Target dead ahead." Businesslike.

I could see Ribeville 15,000 feet below to the left of my
Hurricane's nose, cleverly camouflaged hangars, painted runways to simulate fields, widely dispersed domestic buildings
and stores, the water tower which we had been warned dou-
bled as a light flak post. No point looking for fighters taking
off. They would be airborne already, patrolling somewhere in
the sun to the southeast. That's what I had been told.

The flak thickened as we neared the target, at three-quarter
throttle now, weaving in broad sweeps above and behind the
two formations. I adjusted the intensity of my reflector sight
on the screen—a circle with horizontal lines, center dot, adjust-
able range bars preset to the likely target—and with my thumb
slipped over the safety shield from the gun button.

New sprog. Not an op in my log book. Not a shot fired at
the enemy. But those months of training and practice were
paying dividends now. No more introspection. My mind was
as crisp and clear as this autumn day, my reactions sharp, my
eyes constantly scanning the sky above and behind, occasionally sweeping below to check against a surprise belly attack.

One of the Blenheims in the leading squadron had been hit,
smoke streaming from port engine, banking out of formation
steeply to port and losing height.

"Octave Leader, Octave Red Four. Port engine's had it,
starboard engine nil oil pressure. Will try to make the
coast."

Not a chance in hell, I thought. The coast was fifty miles distant. Before I could do a calculation, the starboard engine caught fire, flames trailing behind, and then—one, two, three —the crew bailed out, distant black dots, briefly streaming white like a contrail, and then the bold circular splash of the open parachute. Brolley-hopping into France. I imagined their landing, the prompt arrival of German troops, the long journey under guard to Stalag Luft something-or-other. Better than falling in small fragments like the last lot.

Behind us, the flak puffs had been so thick that in places they formed uneven splashes in the sky like torn pieces of gray cloth. The bombers had closed up formation for their final run-in, and another was losing height.

"Reindeer Blue One and Two, escort that straggler, over." It was Squadron Leader Taylor's Canadian burr. And two Hurricanes at once detached themselves, losing height to pick up the crippled Blenheim. Three out of twenty-four before they even reached the target.

Then: "O.K., Octave aircraft—bombs away."

Seconds later I caught a glimpse of the bombs landing on the airfield, like hurled gravel into a smooth pond, circular shock waves fanning out from each explosion, then smoke and dust clouds obscuring the target.

Our Hurricanes conformed to the Blenheims' loose turn away from the airfield. They were losing height to gain further speed, and were doing over 250 mph when the 109s came in.

The top cover Spitfires saw them first, and new voices broke in. "I've got him, Sammy!" "Break, Jack, one on your tail!" "Two right above you!" "Oh, Christ!" Dead into the glare of the sun, still 10,000 feet above us, I spotted weaving dots that rapidly enlarged as the German fighters struggled to break through to the vulnerable bombers below. A few seconds later, a single fighter screamed down vertically not a quarter mile away, trailing a thin line of white vapor. It was a Spitfire, and the machine was not going to pull out, its pilot dead or his

controls shot away. I did not wait for the inevitable splash of
the explosion far below as it struck.

Eliot transmitted, "Here they come, boss. Seven o'clock,
three of them. More to follow."

"Break, all Reindeer aircraft—break and mix it. And watch
your goddam tails and everyone else's."

The voices of flight commander and C.O. were reassuring,
calling for steadiness amidst chaos. The scrap was just as I
imagined it would be, the sky suddenly full of 109s—109s with
rounded wingtips, the latest and fastest—wheeling and aileroning, climbing at impossible angles, turning like a ball on a tight
string.

The world was suddenly, briefly, an anarchical world of
glimpses—glimpses of black crosses and wingtips, roundels
and muzzle flashes, a cockpit here (friend or foe?), and the full
length of an underside streaming past in the opposite direction
at a combined speed of over 600 mph.

I was totally bewildered and confused and merely threw my
Hurricane about in desperate climbing turns, then upside
down in a bastard Immelmann, panicked, stalled, began to fall
into a spin. And then, miraculously before me like a stopped
frame in a movie reel gone mad, I saw the complete length of
a 109, from stubby yellow spinner to unbraced tailplane. Right
in front of me. A hundred yards—no, less than that.

I gave it a half ring deflection, pulled the dot through, and
pressed the button in a long burst. It was as if hydraulic drills
were hammering at both my wings as the four big cannon
threw out their shells at a total of forty a second. No steadiness,
no skill, seemed to be needed. The tracers showed that I was
hitting, running the length of the cockpit, below the radio
aerial, clear through the big black cross and the identification
letters P and O, tearing the tailplane to shreds.

I was appalled at my own power of destruction. A beautiful
little 350-mph fighter and its young pilot—all had been reduced
to fragments before my eyes. Some fragments bigger than

others. As I hurled my machine into a stall turn, I saw the
engine and nose falling away and down, its perspective dis-
torted by my angle and speed; then a complete wing, but not
much else identifiable, all disappearing in a faint haze of vapor
and smoke as light as a fleck of cirrus cloud. And I had checked
neither my turn-and-bank, nor my tail. Lucky.

I had killed. I was alive. And I was alone. Not a machine to
be seen anywhere, above or below, to all points of the compass.
I might have fallen asleep at the controls and awakened from
a cruel dream over countryside of irregular fields and woods
and scattered villages—over England, over safety.

Just put her down, anywhere, a voice was saying, and kiss
the earth and thank your Creator and beg for mercy for the sin
of murder. . . .

Then a black puff appeared not a hundred yards in front of
me, and I was back in the real hostile world of enemy territory.
My throttle was already wide open from the combat, the
knurled friction screw on the quadrant tight to give me two
hands for the control column. So I jinked then kicked right-
left-right-right and dived flat out, A.S.I. showing 385 mph,
boost at God-knows-what, my head turning like a ventrilo-
quist's dummy gone mad, and made for the distant line of the
French coast.

I was last in and made a poor landing, and was glad Bruno
was not watching. Not that anyone noticed. The A Flight
pilots were huddled together in a corner of the hut, smoking,
some with feet up on the stove fender, Archy Black with his
spaniel dog on his lap pensively stroking its ears. The Spy was
taking down a report from Eliot, who was twirling his R / T
bayonet plug in one hand and holding a cigarette in the other.
I heard him say, "About forty I'd guess. They'd been mixing
it with the Spits and had their eye in when they got down to
us. . . . Yes, I might have hit one, not sure."

Eliot turned and saw me taking off my kit, unstrapping my
gun. He went on talking to the I.O. for another minute, then
said, "You made it, then? Get hit?"

"I don't think so, sir." He offered me a cigarette from his scarlet packet, which had been crushed by the tight straps across his tunic pocket. I longed for one but refused, knowing that my fingers would twitch and that I could not hold it. Not fear, I told myself. Just cold from my soaked shirt drying on my chest and back. God, how I had sweated!

The Spy said, "Any joy, Mick?"

"Yes, sir. A 109. Destroyed."

The dispersal hut chatter ceased like the needle lifted from a record. But only for about half a second. "You'd better give me a report, then," the Spy said.

Eliot drew on his cigarette then stamped it into the linoleum floor. "Wizard show, Boyd. Anyone see it go in?" And he walked off obviously not believing me. Young sprog who had once tried to get into Training Command? Not likely.

In dices over enemy-occupied land, confirmation of a claim nearly always depended on the automatic camera fixed onto the wing, most pilots who survived being too busy watching the tail of their number one, evading or shooting, to act as witness. The films that day were all processed by 5 P.M. and we biked or walked to the photo Nissen hut where the blackout curtains were drawn and we sat smoking and mocking the projectionist while he got the machine going.

The aircraft number was announced and then the flickering, gray film was screened amid ribaldry. "My God, look at Taffy's shooting!" someone shouted as the 20 mm tracers were shown at extreme range arching high above a 109's tail. Then the C.O.'s two-second burst, from full deflection at about 250 yards to a quarter ring at 50 yards, with chunks of fuselage and tailplane tearing off and finally a blinding flash that filled the screen. "That burnt your eyebrows, boss," one of the flight commanders said.

The show went on for an hour, some of the reels blank, others revealing shooting that varied from marvelous, like the C.O.'s, to downright bad. I waited anxiously for mine in that smoke-filled hut, confident that I would be able to enter my confirmed claim in my log book that evening. Then the projectionist said, "That's the lot, sir."

I wished that the lights had not been switched on. Everyone was talking at once, saying "I tell you, mine hadn't got a chance," "Quit shooting a line, Charlie!"—this from an American due to join one of the Eagle Squadrons next week.

I said to the projectionist, "Where's mine?"

"That's all, sarge. What's your number?"

"I was flying 2075—F-Freddie." He glanced at a sheet, stubby, nicotine-stained forefinger running down the names. "No, nothing, sorry. Duff film, I guess. Happens sometimes."

Eliot was busy talking to the C.O. Pilots brushed past me, hellbent for the pub or movies with some W.A.A.F. Last out was Bill Otway. He was the only one who said anything. "Tough tit, Mick. Come and have a beer."

We all got fairly tight after that show. When I went to bed I told myself for the one hundredth time that it did not matter. *I* knew, that's what mattered. And I saw the film in my mind as it should have appeared, a gray, flickering retake of that 1½ seconds of searing annihilation when I had torn a young German and his fighter to pieces with four Hispano cannon.

Or had I? A sense of guilt, then of revulsion and of outrage in turn raced through my mind. It seemed a long way from Croydon, and the little hut at the bottom of the garden where I made models from balsa wood. I wanted to talk to Vivienne, desperately. But all that I saw that night was a retake and another retake, again and again in my mind, of the 1½ seconds, which no one believed had really happened. And not a bloody wink of bloody sleep, as Jimmy Hanwell would have said.

CHAPTER SEVEN

"This One's Yours, Razor"

I did not see her until early December. The weather was terrible for days on end, and we all got bored and slack sitting around the dispersal smoking, playing cards, and drinking endless mugs of N.A.A.F.I. tea. Once or twice the C.O. told the flight commanders to order us around the perimeter track at the double to shake us up, and one day, in a temporary clearance, I managed to scrounge an engine test. I climbed up through solid cloud for 3,000 feet and burst out into blazing winter sun, though it was not so much fun creeping down again, with the ground suddenly flickering into view through the cloud base, much too close.

But war is nine-tenths boredom and one-tenth terror, as some joker truthfully said, and the boredom of bad weather that kept us on the ground for days on end was demoralizing. Another idea of the C.O.'s to fill in time was to institute aircraft identification competitions between Flights. Models of Heinkel 111s and Junkers 88s, Henschels and 109s, mixed in with Allied aircraft, were set up on cotton hanging from a frame, and we had to name them as quickly as possible from varying distances.

I thought I ought to be good at this, but I never believed—
nor did anyone else—that I would be so outstanding that my
Flight won every time. At the conclusion of our third victory,
with a bottle of whisky as prize, Eliot said in unconcealed
admiration, "My God, Boyd, you really have got razor eyes.
Wasn't it you who spotted the Blenheims the other day on that
op? And that convoy first time up?"

I was now firmly registered as 140's sharpest-eyed pilot, a
fact which was comforting, and was to have far-reaching
consequences. Razor became my squadron nickname, and it
stuck.

The bad weather broke at last, and one evening met. said that
a high was moving in over northern Europe and we could
expect clear skies for a couple of days. So a 2 Group Wing was
ordered to bomb up for a raid on the railway yards at Lille,
with 140 Squadron as close cover, as usual. The whole show
was a dud because of Channel fog. It had already rolled over
northern France like a great white eiderdown as we were
crossing the Channel at 17,000 feet. We could just see the end
of it about fifty miles south, but far beyond the target. So we
did a great wide, sweeping 180-degree turn, with all the bombers keeping very fancy formation, and headed home.

One of the Spitfire boys, their machines making contrails
10,000 feet above us, exclaimed suddenly, "Who'll chip away
the ice if I have to brolley-hop!" and was ordered to shut up.
That was all that was said until we were halfway across the
Channel again when the controller cut in:

"Hullo all Cheeseboard aircraft—big boys go home, the rest
of you set course for Bluebird. I repeat . . ." I checked my code
card. Bluebird was miles away—Malton Green in Essex. Then
I saw the reason. In half an hour the sea fog had spilled north
as well, rolling over Sussex and Kent for almost as far as we
could see, though there appeared to be a faint haze of sunlit
land far to the north.

The bombers were all right. Their base was up in Lincolnshire and they had plenty of fuel. But by the time we got near Malton Green the last gallons would be sloshing about in the tanks.

The sector controller picked us up at extreme range, very faint, a woman's voice. Then suddenly, because of some air freak, it came clear as a bell: "Hullo Cheeseboard, this is Bluebeard. Steer zero-two-zero and reduce to angels five—over—over."

If we had been bounced by jerries then I should have gone for a Burton all right. For a full five seconds I was stunned by Vivienne's voice and the repeated word. And when the C.O. acknowledged, I threw over the switch on the V.H.F. box and added an "over" of my own after his.

Now the day was even more beautiful, with the sun burning off the hoar frost from the fields, which then assumed again their patchwork colors of Essex brown soil and green sheen of autumn-sown corn.

"My God," I shouted into my dead mike, "I may be actually seeing her!"

Then we were in the circuit, gauge needles nudging zero, and landing in loose section formation, on the grass, the runways, perimeter track—anywhere so long as it was good mother earth. It was a shambles for a good ten minutes, with one of the Spits landing with a dead engine, and the troops nearly going mad having to cope with a sudden rush of nearly fifty fighters, fuel bowsers racing about like Dodg'em cars.

There was a flap in the ops room, too, and it was half an hour before I could get Vivienne on the phone. "No, darling," she kept saying until I could have screamed. "No, you know I'd do anything to see you but . . . no, not till this evening. There's a station hop at nineteen hundred. . . ."

Nineteen hundred! What use was that? We'd be airborne in an hour. But it was a day of mixed fortunes all right. The weather south remained clamped down all day, and we were told at teatime that we would be spending the night here. It meant dirty blankets in a cold Nissen hut somewhere, but who cared.

I was there at the hall on the dot, a seething mass of all ranks, male and female, waiting for the hut doors to open, grumbling and singing in the blackout, with the smoke of cigarettes and steaming breath rising above the mob in the half-moonlight.

They were playing "Chatanooga Choo-Choo" when she came in. I was standing with my back to the wall near enough to the door to be sure of spotting her. But I hardly had a chance of savoring the pleasure of seeing her again. It had never crossed my mind that Jo would be with her.

It was not just the presence of Jo; it was also my sister's awful appearance. I was not prepared for that, either. I had heard from my mother that she had been on brief compassionate leave and was dead tired. Now she was working in the same ops room as Vivienne. I had never thought that Jo, of all people, would show the strain like this. She had black rims under her eyes and had lost a lot of weight, and when she recognized me her smile was an effort.

There was an awkward moment as the three of us stood just inside the door, with people brushing past, and the "hallos" said. In ordinary life we would have kissed, and I would have walked off proudly with one on each arm. But this was a sergeant pilot with two W.A.A.F. officers, and even at an informal station dance you could not do more than shake hands. Which we did, awkwardly.

Vivienne said, "She wouldn't have come if it hadn't been for you."

Jo looked at me with that strained smile again and said, with an edge to her voice, "Ah, sisterly love, you see."

I ignored that and said, "You look tired, Jo."

"She's whacked," said Vivienne, "and won't go to the doctor."

"I'm not staying if you go on like this. It's only because I've been on nights."

"And bombed out twice, and three of your girls killed, and . . ."

Luckily a group of Spitfire officer pilots came in at that moment, already full of beer, and swept Jo away. But I got Vivienne in time and guided her into the mob of fox-trotters where rank could hardly be recognized and did not much matter anyway.

"Good old Channel fog," Vivienne said. "I wonder what genius at II Group arranged for you to be diverted here."

"Better still if they had given us some notice and I could have dressed for the occasion." I was wearing an old collarless shirt, an oil-stained silk flying scarf, and seedy battledress that I always wore for flying.

"You look wizard." Near to the band, she had to talk in my ear. "Mick," she shouted, "let's go for a walk. This is terrible."

It was bitterly cold outside and we stood huddled in the shelter of the parachute store tight-clasped for warmth and love. When we stopped kissing she said teasingly, "Ah, love! It survives everything—war, station hops, arctic temperatures."

Through her laughter I heard the air-raid sirens, very distantly on the still, cold air. We waited in silence for the wailing of nearer sirens, but the next siren to sound out was even more distant—as distant as the faint *crrrump* of exploding antiaircraft shells that followed the raiders towards the Midlands.

"You had a busy day last week," Vivienne said. It was rather like my mother saying to my father, before the war, "You had a busy day at the office last week, dear." Except that Vivienne added, "Did you have any joy?"

"Yes, by a bit of good luck," I told her. "But by a bit of bad luck, my camera gun wasn't working. Still, it doesn't really matter."

But she knew that it did matter very much, if only because it looked as if I was just showing off as a sprog pilot on the squadron.

"That's tough luck," she said. She had begun to shiver and we went back, through the double blackout doors, into the hut where the noise was louder, the smoke thicker, the people still more numerous, and the smell of hot bodies more pungent than before. Everything seemed the same only worse. But that was not true, not true at all, for during the brief course of that noisy hop, the history of the world was being nudged on to a new course altogether. And within minutes of our return to the heat and crush, we were being told about it.

The station Squadron Leader Administration, a big man in voice and frame, laboriously made his way up the steps on to the bandstand, indicated to the vocalist that he wanted to speak, and called, "Silence, please, ladies and gentlemen!"

He spoke weightily, as if he himself was the history maker. "I have just learned some important news, which I must pass on to you at once. At seven o'clock this morning, local time, Japanese naval aircraft and submarines attacked without warn- ing the American naval and air bases at Pearl Harbor, Honolulu. Damage to the American battle fleet is very serious, and there is heavy loss of life. The United States has declared war on Japan, and also on Germany. . . ."

The rising murmur which had accompanied these words rose to a cheering crescendo, and the officer could no longer make himself heard.

I glanced at Vivienne, who had come half across the world to fight her war. The loneliness which had haunted Britain and her Commonwealth allies since the fall of France, the sensation of fighting a war without end alone, was already dissolving. My first thought was, "My God, we're going to win after all!"

Vivienne held my hand for a moment, and then I guided her through the milling, shouting crowd towards the counter where I bought pints of beer and N.A.A.F.I. sausage rolls. We made one or two efforts to talk. But I think our hearts were too full, and we were both too tired after our 5 A.M. start to the day. So I said, "Shall we go?" and Vivienne nodded.

We looked for Jo but she had disappeared. "You'd better see

the doctor yourself if she won't go," I suggested, and Vivienne promised that she would.

We kissed goodnight near the entrance to the W.A.A.F. officer quarters. The moon had sunk low in the winter night sky, and there was still the faint rumble of distant bombing or ack-ack. Then it was lost in the nearby roar of a Merlin engine starting up at the dispersal. I was in love, and at the same time I thought my chances of living through the next six months were about as bright as the blackout all around us. In fact for a few seconds I was so carried away with emotion that I stupidly said, "Let's get married—quickly—now."

There was a half-second pause, then Vivienne said lightly, "Now don't get fresh, sergeant, or I'll have to pull my rank on you." But she put her hand gently against my face. The leather of her smart officer's glove smelled sharp yet intimate. "Night night. Over, over."

I tried to grab her for a last kiss but she turned quickly and the darkness folded her away. "Over, over," I called after her disconsolately.

During the next months at West Cowley, like everyone else I learned to adjust myself to a lot of things. These were mostly of a practical and survival nature, which was just as well if you did not fancy getting the chop. Little things, some of them. Like checking the rheostat on the reflector sight just before you dived for the sea or the ground, because you would need increased brightness. Like playing poker in silk inner flying gloves to keep the cards clean and save you 3½ seconds if you were suddenly scrambled.

There were other, more intangible, adjustments, too, and the most important as far as I was concerned was brutally thrusting aside when on ops and even when on readiness, sentimental thoughts and plans concerning Vivienne. Like all very old clichés, the one about love and flying not mixing was as hard-nosed and undeviating as a Mauser bullet.

I had already absorbed one bit of homespun philosophy,

willy-nilly. And that was, "Don't harbor resentments." I had long ago ceased to worry about the 109, and recognized that the only true record was the one in my knowledge and memory. I had not imagined that machine being torn apart by the explosion of my shells. It had really happened. The only thing that mattered, I had continued to tell myself until I believed it, was that I had killed a man at close range, and—like it or not, and I had not liked it—had contributed therefore a tiny pinprick towards the final fatal wound that must destroy the German war machine.

Then, on February 18, a signal came through from Group. It ran something like this: "Message received from undesignated sources in occupied France confirms that wreckage of German fighter fell in area half kilometer north village St. Auberne S & O a.m. 4th November."

I gathered later there was a bit of a post-mortem about this in the C.O.'s office. All I knew was that I was called to the Spy's place after midday dinner, and Eliot was there, too, his piercing blue eyes on me as if I had committed the ultimate flying crime. But it was nothing like that. He snapped, "You can chalk up one after all, Sergeant Boyd. Sorry it's a bit late. This one's yours, Razor." And he handed me the pink bit of paper.

"Thank you, sir." But I was not thanking anyone, really. I just did not feel that it mattered anymore.

Then exactly one week later came the really dread gen—for everyone. "We're converting to bombers," somebody uttered. Hurribombers. Insurrection! "But we're *fighter* pilots!" Applications for postings, all turned down. So one day our kites —every damn one of them—were flown away by a bevy of A.T.A. pilots, mostly women who got booed and hissed and gave as good as they got. And in came the Hurribombers the next day. Mark IIbs, with a bomb rack bulge under each wing, and back to eight machine guns, which were like pellet tubes after 20 mm cannon.

Two days later they were all bombed up with dummy 250-pounders. Eliot pronounced, "Ours not to reason why," tapped out his pipe on the damn-near white-hot coke stove, and told the Flight to get out and start engines.

It was a very hit-and-miss business. We just went in from about 8,000 feet, the steeper the more accurate, used our gun sight, began to pull it through the target at 2 to 3 thousand feet, when we were doing about 400 mph and shaking a bit, pressed the button on the throttle handle, and hauled hard back on the stick, often skimming much too close to the ground or sea.

Dive-bombing had its moments. By contrast with rhubarbs and circuses, ramrods, and sweeps, at least we had a definite task to perform at a prearranged target, usually shipping or railway yards and sidings. We were also escorted by Spitfires or the new American Mustangs, which were beginning to arrive from the States. This was part humiliating (we still thought of ourselves as fighter pilots—the elite!) and part reassuring, because we were slower than ever, inadequately armed, and had to face not only the latest 109 but the new snub-nosed, super-fast, super-maneuverable Focke-Wulf 190.

But we had to look after ourselves all too often, not always successfully. B Flight lost two pilots one afternoon when they were jumped by 190s, both flamers and that was not very nice, and a third who was seen to bail out. We lost one on intruder work, and poor old Bill Otway bought it late in March. I was with him at the time. The very first round of heavy flak from a battery near Boulogne caught him, and there's no worse luck than that. He was only about a hundred yards from me, and I saw him dropping away with his port wing almost all gone, like a falling sycamore seed.

I shouted at him to get out, which was pretty stupid as he was not going to stay in that cockpit from choice. I just hoped to God he was dead because from 15,000 feet it took a long time. Even before he hit the ground I was grieving for his sailor-father and his bitterness and now his grief; and as for me, I felt

my old enemy inside my head stir and threaten before I shut
it out of my consciousness.

Then there was an Easter break in the round of steady ops
and steady losses. Seven days' leave. SEVEN days! A lifetime.
My commission came through the day before I left West Cowley. I had put in for one as a counter-tease at Vivienne after our
last meeting. To my surprise I became Pilot Officer Michael
Boyd R.A.F.V.R. and I took my clothing coupons to a London
tailor on my first day of leave and came out feeling the greenest
sprog of the war. I took the wire band out of my hat behind
a tree in Hyde Park, threw it away, and then punched the hat
around and rubbed it in dust and felt better.

Home was like a small, overdressed, friendly woman. All
those soft, chintz-covered chairs in tiny rooms. I went and
looked in my workshop. My models hanging from strings
were covered in dust, and I was shocked at how crude they
were and how old-fashioned the planes already looked, Harts
and Whitleys and Gladiators.

My mother came back from a shopping trip with an enormous bag, mostly unrationed vegetables. She had managed to
wheedle some sausages out of the butcher on the strength of
the "hero's" return. She was bubbling with energy, cheerful
about the progress of the war—Singapore, Hong Kong, the
Dutch East Indies, and virtually the whole of the Pacific and
Indian Ocean had been taken by the Japanese; and Australia,
India, New Zealand, Moscow, Leningrad and Stalingrad were
all threatened. But my mum thought everything was going
marvelously.

"And what about you, love? Enjoying this new dive-bombing, are you? Must be good fun."

It was a great relief to be able to recount some of my hairier
ops in detail without (seemingly) turning a gray hair of my
mother's head. She loved it all.

Then my father came back, late and tired, from his office,

with the prospect of fire-watching to come. He was very nice and very solicitous. One of the best things about my father was that he was intelligent enough to know that he was a bit of a bore and a depressant, but managed to rise above this disability. "Keeping your chin up," was the cornerstone of his philosophy.

Late, over a precious, stored-away bottle of whisky, he told me about Jo. My mother had been very evasive, but cheerful. "She's not too well at all," my father said as he meticulously filled his pipe. "They sent her here and she just slept and slept and cried."

"Cried!" I exclaimed. "Jo doesn't cry."

"It's a breakdown, Mick. And not a small one. She's really been through it. So she's at a place in Northamptonshire. We're going to visit her next weekend. But the matron says she's not too well and will have to be there for some time."

I was appalled. Tough, inflexible, fast-moving Jo Boyd in a home—an asylum! "Was she jilted?" I asked, for something to say.

"No, they say it was overwork and worry."

CHAPTER EIGHT

Bruno's Spitfire

To return to West Cowley after a week was like reboarding a packed, fast-driven bus full of shouting passengers, most of whom you know, but not very well. There was a well-known poster appeal at the time, "Is your journey really necessary?" It appeared that 140 Squadron's journeys were. Spring appeared to affect Fighter Command with a need to get every aircraft into the air, like migrating birds. We flew every day it was possible to fly. Later, the C.O. explained that it was to impress the Russians, who thought they were doing all the fighting, with the fact that we were hammering the Germans so hard over France that we were tying down a large part of the Luftwaffe.

A week later the C.O. himself went in. He was seen bailing out somewhere south of Rouen so was probably all right. Eliot was made C.O. and at once began to instill an even more offensive spirit into the squadron. We lost three pilots in one week, and I came back from a bombing mission with half my tail gone from a direct hit from a flak ship.

Around August 17 we all had a feeling something big was

brewing up. We were very sensitive to that sort of thing, and the whole R.A.F. was like an electronic web of rumor—ace gen, gen, and duff gen, as it was called. Andy Mitchell, the tall, fair-haired pilot who had arrived on the squadron at about the same time as me, had become a close friend. I liked his dry, quiet humor and resigned cynicism. It was Andy who gave me the ace gen over a whisky in the bar on the evening of the seventeenth.

"We are being overwhelmed by swarms of foreigners tomorrow," he said, staring gloomily at the bottom of his empty glass.

"The invasion at last?"

"Nearly as bad. Thousands of smelly young sprogs in Spitfires. Come to protect us!"

In fact two squadrons of very veteran Spitfire squadrons flew into West Cowley soon after breakfast, all Mark Vs with cannon and clipped wingtips which spoiled their daintiness but made them very fast low down, so the gen had it. "My God, it's 550!" I shouted out loud as I watched the first section of the first squadron in the circuit, wheels down like a ballerina's legs. There were the code letters, A.J., Bruno's mob!

I knew he had a thick ring on his sleeve now, Flying Officer Bruno Caswell. But the D.F.C. ribbon was a staggering surprise.

"Why the hell didn't you tell me?" I demanded.

He looked down at me from his lofty elevation and threw the Mae West (which had concealed the decoration) on to a chair. "Oh that—it's a dummy. To provoke the girls. Works, too."

We went into the mess and had a second breakfast. "Come on, love, make it two eggs," he pleaded. "Tomorrow I'm laying down my life for King and Empire."

The W.A.A.F. giggled, looked left and right, and then slipped them on to Bruno's plate. "Thanks. We must go out to the movies tonight. Nice?"

Later, as we cleaned up our plates Bruno said, "All we were told was that leave was canceled, we were confined to station, and we were coming here. And it's not, repeat, not the invasion."

I said, "Well, it must be something big."

And so it was. The biggest air battle of the whole war. Anywhere, any time.

"500s?"

"Yes, 500s."

"You're kidding."

"It's bloomin' murder, Spy."

We went out into the dusk light after the briefing, and they were not kidding. The armorers had finished their work and were hugging pints of tea, squatting on their bomb trolleys and smoking reflectively. When we arrived in an indignant body, they watched our reactions with sardonic amusement. Relations between pilots and the troops were always good, but there were no false emotions, let alone hero-worshiping nonsense. They reckoned we were doing a job, too. They worked harder at nastier work and were paid less. We got the glamour, the privileges, the rank, the money and most of the risks.

And now, there was the armorers' handiwork. Under each wing, neatly hanging from its rack, was a bomb twice the weight of any we had carried before.

A sergeant from Melbourne asked the armorer corporal, "Hey, cobber, has anyone tested these ruddy wings with half a ruddy ton under 'em?"

"Don't worry, sarge, it'll encourage you to take off smoothly."

Later, I went for a stroll with Bruno down to the dispersal and climbed into his Spitfire's cockpit. It was much more cramped than the Hurricane's, and I asked him how he fitted.

"They had to do some surgery with the seat struts," he said. "And I have to keep my hair cut short."

He seemed as cheerful and confident as ever, a seasoned fighter pilot with a couple of 109s and a Focke-Wulf 190 to his name. He was obviously glad to see me, but told me that he was anxious to get this job over and return to North Weald where he had a W.A.A.F. officer with red hair and a cracking figure and . . . and . . . The same old Bruno.

We took off before dawn, and before the Spitfires. It seemed to take twice as long to get off the ground, and the Hurricane felt even more wallowy with this half-ton load. We did not have to climb, and Eliot led us all the way across the Channel at nought feet. Our target was a battery of guns north of Dieppe, which the Canadian army was raiding on a big scale. The Spy had called it "an invasion rehearsal."

It was not going to be a surprise one. We saw that long before we reached the target. A ship was on fire off the French coast, lighting up everything for miles around, including our landing craft. The C.O. led us around the brightest light, and a mile from the white cliffs; we climbed as steeply as we could, taking the first of the flak as we did so.

We crossed in at 3,000 feet, with everything and the kitchen sink coming up at us, the 40 mm tracer half-blinding us with its multiple arcs of color from every side: very pretty for a fireworks party, very ugly when the cracks of the explosions were near enough to drown the engine and wind roar. I managed to pick out the heavily camouflaged battery of six guns, just back from the cliff edge, conforming with the P.R.U. photograph we had been shown at briefing. A few seconds later, Eliot, jinking about all over the sky, changed course and called out, "Target at three o'clock. Going in *now.*"

This was no time for hanging about. I saw him turn upside-down and begin his dive into the holocaust of flak, followed by the rest of his section. Someone was on fire, and I heard a voice shouting out—I think it was Archy Black's—"Get out, Red Three, for Christ's sake get out."

I was too busy to look around. My section leader went

down, then his number two, then Bill Mason, and it was my turn. Stick hard over, the horizon (if you could call it that in this light) swinging through 180 degrees, then hard back to settle the dive at about 70 degrees, the flak coning us all the way down.

All the way down? Well, for about three seconds from our height, then I was steadying the center dot of the sight on the gray-brown smudge against the grass, picking out a few details —the stubby muzzles of the big guns, running figures, a vehicle moving between the concrete emplacements, a brief squirt with my guns to help keep their heads down, and then squeeze the bomb release, and both hands on the stick to haul out.

The cliff edge shot past under my wings. "Bye-bye ruddy France!" an Australian voice was shouting, and was shut up firmly by Eliot. I threw the stick forward again, kicking left— right—left rudder and aileroning like mad. Anything to throw off the horribly accurate aim of those flak gunners.

Seven of us got into some sort of formation about five miles out and well north of the landing craft and their escort, who would have shot us out of the sky they were so trigger happy. There was more light now, and in fifteen more minutes, Beachy Head showed up like a great white Welcome signboard, all 800 feet of it.

The air was full of the usual shouts of combat, the volume and frequency of orders and oaths louder than I had ever heard. At briefing we had been told that there would be sixty-three single-engine fighter squadrons operating in support of the raid, far more than at any time in the Battle of Britain, and every one of them seemed to be airborne and on the same wavelength as we crossed over and got into the West Cowley circuit.

Two of 140 came back later, three more did not come back at all. As the nearest friendly airfield to Dieppe, we got a lot of wrecks, too. Three Spitfires came in, with wheels up, and the crash wagon never stopped.

The N.A.A.F.I. van came round at 10 A.M. We were all refueled and bombed up again awaiting another target, and we queued up with the troops for tea and a bun. Everybody was talking more than usual. Sort of mass hypertension, I suppose. It happened after any really big show, especially if there was more to come. Even the troops would put out their cigarette butts before they were half smoked. You could sense the pressure, almost smell it, blended with the usual dispersal stench of glycol, oil, 100-octane fuel, and hot bodies in dirty blue overalls.

One pilot—a Canadian—who had just got back in a flak-holed Mustang said he had seen the Dieppe beach from low level, and there was not a tank that was moving. "Poor sods!" he exclaimed of his countrymen and lit a cigarette with shaking hands.

Another Spitfire came in just as I had finished my mug. It came in downwind from the west, which was odd, and someone fired off a red Very to warn the pilot. But the Spitfire came on, steadily, engine sounding healthy and nicely ticking over, wheels and flaps down, all very tidy. I could read the squadron letters on the fuselage, A.J. One of Bruno's mob. Now I saw it was trailing a fine vapor from the engine. Glycol leak? And now Razor eyes could actually pick out the three swastikas painted under the cockpit.

Of course, it was K-King, Bruno himself. Silly sod landing downwind. I would take a pint off him for that. But true to form, he held back beautifully, just a foot or two off the runway as he lost speed, and then touched down.

"A perfect three-pointer." Bruno's voice came back from our schooldays. He would be pleased with that, with half the station watching.

The little Mark V Spitfire came to a halt, almost at the end of the runway. It did not move. It just stayed there, prop ticking over, hood open. I could see Bruno's head, almost on a level with the top of the windshield. And like his kite, it did not move.

A second Very went up, arched over the machine. Get off

the runway, it was warning. Get clear. But still the Spitfire did not move.

What in God's name was going on? I grabbed the nearest bicycle. It was marked W.O. Partridge in roughly painted letters. I don't understand why I noticed. Warrant Officer Partridge was the station armorer and very fierce but I would have borrowed the C.O.'s car at that moment. I pedaled as fast as I could along the perimeter track towards the stationary Spitfire, prop still turning—like my mind: What was Bruno doing? Why did he just *sit* there? What had happened to him?

Others were running towards the plane and I heard Eliot's motorbike starting, and the sound of voices. I was the first there. The Spit looked fine. There were the usual black stains behind the exhaust stubs, and the muzzle covers had been blown off the cannon, proving he had been in action. All OK Or was it? I was about to call out to him when I noticed something under the fuselage, and raced around to the other side.

Now overcome by horror, I recognized the deception. Bruno must have died as he touched down, saving his aircraft. At least three shells had torn into the starboard side of the fighter, wantonly ripping the alloy panels and rib structure apart, exposing Bruno and his terrible wounds—too terrible to describe—all down his, and his Mark V Spitfire's, right side. Here, before me like the devil's offering, was the awful reality of my worst fears—the fears I thought I had finally defeated since Bruno and I together, in our schooldays, had watched that Hurricane crash at Croydon.

I screamed "Ambulance—for God's sake send the ambulance!" as I stumbled from my bicycle, and drew my revolver, firing three shots into the air to add three times over to the urgent need for help.

The sound of the explosions brought me back to reality, and at the same time I felt a hand on my shoulder and heard Eliot's voice: "Steady, Razor," and I returned the gun to its holster

with the three live rounds still in their chamber, just as I was
to find them all these years later.

I was so numbed with shock and grief that I went into the
second show of the day, dive-bombing German reinforce-
ments coming up the roads into Dieppe, with such abandoned
fatalism that it was a miracle I survived. I did not bother to jink
in the flak, and when we were bounced on the way back by
half a dozen FW 190s, I hardly bothered with them either. We
were all saved by a squadron of Spits that fought it out with
the Luftwaffe and drove them off.

That evening the wind blew up, heavy cloud filled the sky
—funeral black for Bruno and all the other pilots and all the
hundreds of Canadians who had died on the Dieppe beaches
that day. Still numbed, I managed to get through to Vivienne
on the telephone. The line was awful, and we did not say
much. I just told her Bruno had bought it, and what a bloody
day it was. I could hardly hear what she said. But it was a
comfort to hear her voice. Then I got through to my mother
to warn her that Bruno's parents would be getting a telegram.
"No, I'm OK. Yes, I was over there a couple of times. I'll be
all right, Mum. I'm a survivor."

"Of course you are, Mick."

The tall, rangy figure of Bruno haunted me after Dieppe, his
smiling, smooth-skinned face, his long-fingered hands as able
with women as with a Spitfire's controls, his deep laughter and
the serious emotional note that was sounded at the mention of
his current love affair. He was the person I least expected to
be killed, and when he was, the expectation of dying violently
myself at once became more real. Only in death did I realize
how much I had admired him.

Dieppe, and Bruno's death, changed a great many things for
me. If they could get Bruno, then I had a struggle on my hands;
and I felt that he would have been pleased to see me fight as

he had fought, and survive. "Come on, we can't lose!" I could hear him saying as if we were going in to the final set as partners in the vital Surrey Schools Tennis Championship.

This was all unspoken, of course, even to Vivienne when I next saw her. These things you sorted out for yourself, usually in the brief waking moment before the W.A.A.F. brought you in your early morning cup of tea, or in the darkness of the station cinema, almost the only times when you felt alone in the noisy communal life of a squadron.

At the end of '42, we were sent up north, farther away than ever from Vivienne, and had a quiet cold winter in Morayshire in Scotland. There we got our new fighters, and "not before it's time," as the C.O. remarked. We were almost the last operational Hurricane squadron in the U.K., but they had become suicide crates against the latest German flak and fighters.

"First deliveries next week," Eliot confided over a beer before lunch in early January. He had been down south with a couple of others on a familiarization course. I asked him what he thought of it. "Like an ill-mannered overweight Hurricane," he replied.

CHAPTER NINE

The Dodgy Op

The Typhoon was from the same stable, the same design team as the Hurricane. But it was an all-metal machine, with thick canted wings, a great air intake like a swollen chin, and a new engine. The engine *was* the Typhoon, an incredibly complicated 24-cylinder in H-configuration with sleeve valves and a two-speed supercharger. The Typhoon—the Tiffy—was being pressed into service without a full test program because nothing could catch the latest German fighters. It was paying the price. We had heard that so many had been lost in mysterious circumstances that it had for a while been prohibited from flying over the sea. The troubles had been traced to fumes seeping into the cockpit, and to tails falling off in a dive. Now tails had been reinforced, and pilots used oxygen at all times, regardless of height.

Inevitably, speed was what we wanted to know about. "Four hundred, plus a bit more," Eliot told us. "No good above 20,000, but nothing'll catch her low down."

The Focke-Wulfs were doing about 360 on their tip and run raids on coastal towns at that time, and early Typhoon squadrons had been catching them easily. But Eliot was right: the beast was a handful after the Hurricane, and the torque created by the 2,000 plus horsepower and three-bladed prop caused her to swing at takeoff like an uncontrollable stallion.

But for acceleration and speed, there was nothing to touch the Tiffy in early 1943. Then in March the blow was struck that was to alter the course of the war, and my life.

The adjutant called me to his office one evening. The C.O. was there, and the station commander. As a still-green pilot officer, I felt seriously lacking in rings on my sleeves in this company, and said so, wondering what terrible crime I had committed.

"It's all right," Eliot said, blue eyes twinkling like sapphires in the light of the naked bulb. "You're going to get some more rings in a few days."

I glanced at the station commander, a beefy, red-faced regular wearing ribbons from the campaigns between the world wars. "They call you 'Razor'—is that right, Boyd?"

"I'm afraid so, sir. Makes me feel like one of those gangs at the races before the war."

"Well, you've obviously got exceptional eyesight and are way ahead of anyone else on aircraft recognition."

The adjutant made notes while the other two officers explained that Fighter Command was forming a Special Aircraft Recognition Unit, mainly for P.R.U. pilots. These types photographed targets, from German gun defenses to bomb damage of cities and factories after a raid, from heights of zero feet to 40,000 feet. And I was to take command as chief instructor with the rank of acting flight lieutenant.

I moaned and begged, and of course it was no use. And later I reflected on the irony of the fact that two years ago I was trying to pluck up courage to keep off operations, and now I was furious at the prospect of being prevented from returning to the fighting front. All because of Bruno? No, I was hardening up in one way, and also becoming more humble; losing a sense of the importance of my own life when so many other pilots a great deal more worthwhile than I was were being killed.

For five months I commanded a curious little unit in the grounds of Bentley Priory, Fighter Command H.Q. near London, with a course of six pilots at a time, training them with silhouettes and briefly screened photographs of enemy and Allied aircraft taken from odd angles, until they were nearly as quick as I was. It was tedious, repetitive work. The only advantage was that it was only forty minutes to the center of London, and about once a month Vivienne and I could contrive to meet. She was a flight officer now, so we both had two rings on our sleeves. Between us, we also had enough money to dance in night clubs and indulge ourselves in the better restaurants.

One night when we were dancing in the smoky darkness of Hatchetts, Vivienne said, "You miss flying, don't you, Mick?"

I agreed. "It's like a drug. You feel trapped on the ground. Like ancient man before he learned to ride a horse."

"And ops? Do you miss the fighting?"

I had thought about this a great deal since I had been given this quiet job. Now I said, "After a bit you give up wanting things and not wanting them. You get fatalistic, I suppose. Do you remember in the Blitz people used to say about the bombs, 'If it's got your name on it, it'll get you. If it hasn't, it won't.' "

We danced in silence for a moment. The small floor was packed and we kept bumping into other couples. Then she said, "It doesn't stop me wanting you not to go back on to ops. I reckon you've done your whack."

Two days later a signal ordered me to Ford, a station in Sussex I had flown from once or twice in the past. There seemed to be some urgency, and I couldn't for the life of me think why anyone could need *me* in a hurry.

Traveling was different for an officer. First-class warrant, a

suitcase instead of a kitbag, a driver who saluted to meet you.
And straight to the officers' mess. It was past midnight and
there were only two or three people about. One of them got
up when I came in out of the blackout, blinking in the light.

"Michael Boyd? Ah, yes, I'm the adjutant." He was a severe-
looking, prissy fellow with a thin mustache. "Yes, we've got
a special job for you, if you want it. The sector I.O. will tell
you all about it. He has stayed up especially to meet you."

He had. And, my God, there was a guard outside his office!
I had never seen anything like it. "What's going on?" I asked
nervously. The adjutant had left and there were just the two
of us. "This looks all very hush. What's it all about?" I asked
again.

Most spies were good blokes. They had to be to work well
with the pilots and get all the gen out of them after a show
when you were often bad-tempered or tired or both. This one
was called Spurling, a squadron leader with a rich Yorkshire
accent, and as he spoke I had to keep telling myself that this
was serious and that he was not the music-hall comic his voice
hinted at.

Spurling went straight to the point. "We're getting gen out
of Germany that the Luftwaffe's got a new fighter coming
along. A twin-engined job." Twins were all the rage in the late
1930s, but had gone out of fashion when it was seen that they
were no match in combat with a single-engined machine.

"There's a development branch called the TLR / FL-E, and
don't ask me what that stands for in Hun language." He pronounced it "Hoon." "They've got two prototypes, and we
know where one of them is and how we can get at it."

"How do you mean 'get at it'?" I asked.

"It's within range, and we want it photographed."

"Within range of what?"

"Of a Tiffy." Spurling opened the safe in a corner of the
office and brought out a map of northern France. There was
a small red cross marked southeast of Alençon and north of Le

Mans. Someone had inked in carefully the name "Bosquet," and Spurling placed his index finger beside it. "Twenty-four hours ago it was parked on the south side of this airfield."

"You must have spies everywhere, sir."

"We have friends in France, if that's what you mean. It may have left by now, it may be under cover." He produced a standard P.R.U. photograph of the airfield taken from around 25,000 feet. It showed the nearby village after which the airfield was named, several typical straight French roads, the railway line leading south to Le Mans.

I asked, "Do you have any idea what this prototype looks like?"

Spurling went back to the safe. "This is drawn from a number of reports we've had—a composite picture, not necessarily very accurate." It was done with a pen and black ink, very firmly and skillfully, showing a twin-engined machine with a chunky fuselage, swept wings, the cockpit unusually far back in the fuselage, an orthodox single-fin tail, and a tricycle undercarriage.

"Well, that's quite specific," I said. "But why hasn't the artist put in the props?" They were big engines, set under the wings, but looked very naked without propellers.

Spurling chuckled with satisfaction. "Because there aren't any. It's a jet."

That silenced me for a moment. "A what?"

I was then given a brief rundown on the gas turbine engine, with technical words like "thrust" and "centrifugal," to which I commented irreverently, "You mean it's *blown* along?"

"Yes, sort of. And fast."

"How fast? Over 400?"

"Add a hundred."

"You mean over 500?"

"Yes, well over."

This silenced me again. More than a hundred miles an hour faster than the Tiffy. I understood with a nasty mental lurch that this machine must indeed be very hush, and could be a war winner. But what had it got to do with me? I put this question to Spurling, who sat down at his desk, looking at me quizzically and turning a pencil round and round like a mockery of a propeller.

"We want you to photograph it, Flight Lieutenant Boyd— Razor Eyes. And blow it up if you have time."

I did not want to sound as if I was looking for reasons for not doing this, but I did ask what was the matter with low-level P.R.U.

"The reason," said Spurling in his rich northern voice, "is that you're top identification pilot, according to our information. If it is at Bosquet there'll only be a split second to pick it out from any other parked machines and photograph it from nought feet. If you do get a picture of it, we want it safely delivered back here, and only the Tiffy is fast enough to guarantee to get away from anything the Hun puts up to shoot you down."

"Except this thing," I mentioned sardonically, pointing at the drawing. Then I looked at the map again and did a quick calculation. "But it's over two hundred miles each way," I said. "That's beyond a Tiffy's range."

"Not this one. We had it prepared last month for something like this. I'll show it to you." And he did. It was in a corner of a hangar behind a canvas screen, and I thought again how like a great crouching cheetah the Tiffy was. There was a guard on duty here, too. "You're taking this whole business quite seriously," I said lightly.

There was no light note in Spurling's answer. "*Very* seriously. One day we've got to invade the Continent. It's the only way we can win the war. And you can only invade when you've won control of the air, as the Huns learned in 1940, and did not succeed. With a thousand jets against us, or even five hundred, we wouldn't stand a chance in hell, not with all the American landing craft and tanks and troops. . . ."

This Typhoon was unlike any I had seen. For extra speed, every rivet had been hand-filed down, two cannon and the armor-plate had been removed to save weight, and the engine had been uprated to produce an extra 200 horsepower, so Spurling told me. The camera was fitted behind a flush square of glass in the machine's belly, and two large cigar-shaped objects were secured beneath the wings. When I asked if I was supposed to bomb the damn thing after I had photographed it, Spurling bent down and tapped one of the objects with his knuckles. It did not sound at all like a bomb. "That'll give you an extra hour's flying time. Use the fuel first then jettison 'em. That's why they're called drop tanks."

"You've thought of everything."

"I hope so." He came out from under the wing. The light was rather dim in this corner of the hangar, but I believed I could just identify a quizzical expression on his face. Or could I? Was it only that I expected him to have a quizzical expression? I told myself severely that I'd better be quicker with my identification, when it comes to mystery fighters.

"Your call sign's 'Juno,'" Spurling said and laughed hoarsely. "A stately goddess, protectress of woman. That seems about right for this job." He suddenly turned and marched off towards the gap in the screen like a sentry on duty. "Right, Boyd, you'd better get some gear together," he called out over his shoulder. "Met. says it'll be clear at dawn so we don't want to hang about."

Dawn! He meant *this* dawn, today? He did mean today. I realized that I had about four hours to brief myself for the longest, dodgiest, lowest, most critical show I was ever likely to undertake. And no sleep.

CHAPTER TEN

Juno's Show

There were two fitters holding one of the propeller blades. I could just see their outline in the dimmed light from the part open door of the hangar. When I called out "OK," they drew down the blade, reached up for the next one, and with a good deal of cursing succeeded in hand-turning the massive engine through three revolutions.

Juno indeed! Everything about the Tiffy was violent and brutish and unstately. Its very presence induced cursing and noise. Even my shout of "Stand clear!" was unnecessarily loud, my voice echoing in the dark against the tall steel hangar doors.

Start lever to Start. Throttle lever to the stop position. Start lever to Normal. I watched the fuel pressure gauge on the dully illuminated right side of the instrument panel rise to 2 pounds per square inch as I primed the carburetor. Ignition On. Five pumps with my right hand with the cylinder primer. My God, the complexity! Before my first Tiffy flight, my flight commander had warned, "Remember, getting a 30,000-ton battleship under way is bloody simple compared with this."

I selected a cartridge, pressed the boost and start buttons together, causing a sharp explosion—sharp enough to turn the engine over and send gouts of flame from the exhaust stubs on both sides of the nose. In the end, the Sabre engine started on the third cartridge, with a mixture of vapor and exhaust smoke engulfing the length of the machine. The cloud drifted away, and the engine settled down at 1,000 rpm to a steady rumble no louder than an express train in a tunnel. I crossed my arms to indicate chocks away, and taxied the Tiffy clear, swinging the tail from side to side with brakes and rudder to give myself some visibility ahead.

Because the figure and face and voice of Bruno still often came to my mind, even now a year after he was chopped, I imagined his comments on this steamroller of a fighter after his beloved Spitfire. "Talk about bull in a china shop—it's like a tank with jammed open throttle at the vicar's tea party." Something like that.

But Bruno would have enjoyed the thought of this show. On his own at nought feet. Two and a quarter hours spanning the dawn. Seeking out one plane in one corner of one airfield in the whole of France's 213,000 square miles. He would have loved it!

And me? I had been drinking coffee all through my self-briefing with maps and photos, but my mouth was as dry as a Sahara dune, and my stomach felt as if I had drunk eight pints of beer and then been sick. But there was nothing I could do —sweet sodding bloody nothing, as Jimmy Hanwell would have put it—except press on. I might have been going over the top on the first day of the Battle of the Somme, a subaltern with a loaded revolver behind me, the revolver *not* for the enemy.

There was nothing to savor—only thirst and sickness. Nothing to savor except a faint glimmer of expectation, no brighter than this predawn light. When this show was over, I would be thankful and relieved and . . . Somehow I would talk to Vivienne and tell her that the worst of the war was over, for me at least, there could never be a show like this again, and now we must celebrate by getting married.

But the return, intact, to this airfield was so distant in time, so remote in likelihood, it was not worth a passing thought.

What I needed to think about was getting this right. Brakes locked with the Tiffy at right angles to the runway. Cockpit check, everything from oil inlet temperature to prop control, flaps at 30 degrees. Then transmit for permission to take off, a green Aldis flashed from the watch tower, and the runway lights went on.

I pushed the throttle lever steadily through its quadrant, and the massive power became pressure against my back, and the ever swifter flick of runway lights past the cockpit, the familiar torque swing to the right, the easy lift of the tail with 3,700 rpm and +7 boost, and then the lift-off, the A.S.I. needle moving like a second hand, to 125.

Undercart up, door windows closed, ease back to 3,000 revs and flaps up at 300 feet. To get this ten-ton brute into the air at all seemed a negation of the laws of gravity. But here we were at 500 feet on a clear dark night, with the usual spatter of stars above and a blackness that gave only the faintest of horizons below. Someone had left a bedroom window uncurtained in Chichester, and a car on the main road reflected a faint spread from its hooded lights. And that is all there was to be seen of the city, although a train heading towards it cast a red glow from its firebox and the trailing smoke showed faint gray-white against faint gray-black.

I set 181 degrees on the compass between my knees, turned south, lost height down to a hundred feet over the sea off Selsey Bill, and set prop pitch, mixture, and revs for most economical consumption. Ninety-seven miles to the French coast. A shade under half an hour. Ops had decided that I should stick to the deck all the way, below radar-seeing height, crossing in between the fishing villages of Le Croixville and Eyneport. According to Command confidential maps, there was a battery of heavy flak a mile inland but that could not touch me at 100 feet. And some medium flak—mostly 40 mm it was thought—just east of Eyneport, but with accurate landfall and surprise on my side, I should miss this too.

The white-flecked wavetops whipped by under the wings, soporific but always threatening, forcing my mind to fight against becoming mesmerized. I had seen people cartwheel in, catching a wingtip and disappearing in a riot of spume like an exploding naval shell. But every wave, every second, brought a glimmer more of dawn.

The engine labored on, grumbling deeply like a held-back thoroughbred longing to stretch itself and show its pace. Its steady beat was like the static and the far-away crackle of disembodied voices in my headphones, radio ops testing their TR1133s on some distant airfield back in England.

A Royal Navy motor torpedo boat, crescent bow wave evidence of its speed, loomed up and was gone before identification signals could be exchanged. My eyes ranging constantly from compass needle to A.S.I. glanced again at the illuminated clock. In five minutes I should be looking for a smudge of landfall.

It came up after four minutes, dead on course, a squat lighthouse on a low cliff, rising land behind, darker gray against the dark gray of the southern sky. It was 5:17 A.M., and some French families were about to be woken up early. I eased the stick a shade forward to hug the sea closer, feeling like an animal crouching against discovery. I opened up to 240 A.S.I., braced to jink at the first round of gunfire.

None came. The French cliffs tore towards me. The tide was out. I saw a blur of anti-invasion camouflaged gun emplacements, coils of wire on the beach—a replica of the English shoreline—and then I was lifting the nose, quickly but very lightly, easing my Tiffy over the lip of the cliff a quarter mile from the lighthouse.

Nothing, absolutely nothing. I could have been entering the

land of the dead. Empty roads, empty meadows, farmhouses that might have been abandoned, depopulated villages, no stock in the fields for several miles, then a single herd of sheep, right beneath me, belatedly scattering like sea before a prow.

Five minutes later I picked up the Tougues River, a mile before I should have done, and adjusted a couple of points south. The land was hilly around this part of Normandy and the compass needle swung like the turn-and-bank as I pulled my Tiffy over hills and down into narrow valleys below the treetops on either side.

Merlerault gave me my next landmark. An oblique briefing photograph had shown me a clear silhouette of the town, with its church's unusually tall spire. I was deep into France, dead on course, and already having to take the routine precaution of telling myself, loud and clear, "This is *not* a piece of cake," knowing like the veteran I had become that cockiness was the short way to the butcher's block.

And just as well, too, I told myself with satisfaction thirty seconds after that. Suddenly, tracers were pursuing me like all the hounds of hell. Not pursuing me, shooting past after very marginally missing me. I began jinking like mad, hoping to throw them off, knowing that at my height I could not be in range for more than seconds.

They persisted. And in short bursts, which told me the story my mirror had failed to reveal. Something *was* on my tail. Oh God—two of them! Razor Eyes identified them at once as F.W. 190A-4s, stubby radial engines with a knack of aileroning out of anything. But Razor Eyes had not picked them up until they opened fire, and he should have done so before . . .

This was also bad luck on a mountainous scale. They must have been on routine patrol and picked me up by chance, for there had been no time to scramble fighters and vector them on to me in the time I had been over France.

I combined an all-my-strength starboard turn with a thumb stab at the tank jettison knob. The drop tanks were not yet half empty, but there was no time—absolutely no time—to calculate whether I had enough fuel to get me home because two Luftwaffe pilots of some skill were also trying to stop me getting home. The loss of my underwing burdens transformed my Tiffy, and seemed to please her. She was, in truth, a much maligned beast, for the fact was that, when pressed, the Tiffy was not only supremely fast but responsive to the controls— quite maneuverable in fact.

The two 190s and I played tag around a larch copse, twice around a village (scattering figures in the street, so the place *was* alive). Then I dummied to starboard, turned to port instead past an elderly oak tree, and with everything screaming, went east down a valley and let the simple, unanswerable advantage of speed take me away from these hounds.

I was safe, and miles off course and had lost something like sixty gallons. The old iron beam—the single-seat pilot's railway guide—saved me. I followed one railway east, resisting the temptation to blow up a train that I met, joined a southerly line that I recognized was only five miles west of my track, which I picked up two minutes later, bang over the head of a blue-smocked farmer whose barn happened to be on my course. It was light enough now for him to spot my English red, white, and blue wing roundels, and he waved me on encouragingly.

Now I could do some calculating, between avoiding high tension cables, telegraph posts, and tall trees and churches. My two main tanks were showing almost full, forty gallons each, minus what I had used for takeoff and the encounter with the 190s. At 100 gallons an hour at 3,000 rpm, that would take me . . .

I had the miles marked off in units of ten along my course on the map. Then another seventy plus gallons in the nose tanks for getting home: that could last me over an hour—say seventy-five minutes if I could keep the boost down to + 1 and rpm to 2,300.

But for how much of the return journey would I be able to

toddle along at 210 mph or so? Answer: with half the Luftwaffe in northern France looking for me, not much.

There were railway sidings at Mortagne, great black locomotives blowing off steam, white faces of *cheminots*, railway workers, staring up, and gone almost before the retina could register them. South of the town, a flash of light to port caused me to kick left rudder in defensive reaction. It was only the first segment of rising sun beaming clear across Europe and instantly casting the longest shadow until—until sunset, a sunset I would *not* be seeing if I didn't keep my head better. Yes, "If you can keep your head when all about you are losing theirs." All very well, Mr. Rudyard Kipling. But they're not likely to lose theirs, just waiting for me to come; and I could imagine the single plot moving across the German ops room maps, fighters being scrambled at Lassay, Bazoches, and St. Paterne, gunners on their saddle seats spinning their *Flakvierlings*—multiple barrels. Especially on the northern outskirts of Le Mans, my dummy target. There had been a bombing raid on the Renault works there two days earlier and it would be a natural assumption that a low level P.R.U. would be photographing the damage.

Instead, five miles short where the main road meets the secondary road to Biercy, I did a 115-degree turn to port, following the main road northeast, bang into the fat great red sun, now ten degrees above the horizon.

"Take your choice," Spurling had said. "But I'd rather have the sun in the gunners' eyes when I'm leaving than coming." And so would I.

The sweat was dripping steadily, dividing like a stream around my mask. I hated flying with goggles but I had to pull mine down to keep the salt out of my eyes. I was wearing only a battledress under my Mae West but I could feel the sweat coursing down my side, too, held by the pressure of my harness and then creeping on down to my waist. "The Tiffy is very hot to fly low down—all that engine, y'know." That was the warning to first-timers. But it was not all *this* hot. This was a very special case of blue funk or tension, depending on how you cared to read the symptoms.

Never mind about reading symptons. There was something more important to read: a sign beside the road, pointing right. "Bosquet 7.6 km." That was right. Just under five miles, a bit to the right, the airfield a mile from the village, the jet prototype on this side, pray to God unmasked by trees or camouflage netting. Straight over at twenty feet, camera clicking its magic way at how-many-frames-per-second. And then out. Life could be as neat and tidy as that.

It was not, though. First there was an army convoy, not a big one, but because they got hammered quite often on rhubarbs in northern France their gunners were alert. They were already firing as I caught sight of the olive-drab camouflaged vehicles—armored cars and soft-skinned trucks—and at once kicked rudders to skid and yaw my Tiffy. I opened up to over 3,000 rpm, ducked down even lower, saw tracers whisking across my nose, felt a slight twitch in my port wing and saw a series of holes in a neat line, each with its circular surround of ragged raw metal.

An R.D.F. tower was the first clue to the proximity of Bosquet. Then some landing beacons, cleverly camouflaged huts, a scattering of personnel vehicles. From the P.R.U. photograph, I could see exactly where I was, aileroned slightly to starboard to pick up the correct line, slipped the safety cover off the gun button, and activated the camera release.

There were aircraft in sight, parked in splinter bays, fuel bowsers moving among them, camouflaged runway beyond, administration and domestic buildings on the far side. The light was perfect, the sun not too glaring for me but very glaring for gunners when I shallow-climbed.

I banked fiercely left and right on the approach. So much to register, so little time to register it, at over 300 mph. I could identify a pair of old trimotor Junkers 86s, a big four-engined

Focke-Wulf, a clutch of Fiesler Storches, aphidlike on their
ridiculous undercarts, inevitably some 109s, their hinged canopy hoods thrown back, fitters at work on their engines.

The place was like a display of every Luftwaffe operational
machine, pages wrenched from a photo manual, bewildering
in their range, and I was over and past, skimming the side of
the runway with the first light flak coning in on me. No sign
of the jet; every sign that I was shortly to be blown up. There
was 40 mm coming down at me from a tower now, adding to
the fireworks, the shells making pretty sparks smack in front
of my windshield, and on both sides, too. I yawed and jinked
about as best I could, but there was a limit to evasive action at
twenty feet.

Every damn machine there was familiar. All except one. It
was a Messerschmitt 110, or 210, at first glance, having an engine
overhaul. Then it was nothing of the kind. The engines were
too big, and the absence of airscrews was not caused by their
removal. There were not supposed to be any. Like Spurling's
drawing.

And suddenly everything was wrong, and everything right
about that machine. It was next to a pair of old Heinkel 111s,
like aging parents protecting their precocious son. And there
was a tarpaulin sheet over the tailplane, but not where it mattered up in the nose.

Right, so here it was. But the agony was that I was already
past it, and not even the most maneuverable machine could
turn towards it now. I would have to go around again, in
defiance of the old saying that one pass on a low level target
was madness, a second suicide.

The heavy and light stuff followed me all the way, into sun
and out of sun, and from 200 feet as I assessed my bearings
ready to come in head-on, I could see a couple of 109Fs taking
off, downwind but they wouldn't care. Under other circumstances, I would have spared them a few rounds. Now I had
to concentrate single-mindedly on my target, the twin-engined
baby without props that could do 525 mph straight and level.

Could change the face of aerial warfare. Could leave my super-stripped Tiffy as if stalled. Could be photographed in detail if I just had the nerve to stay straight and level and *not* be shot down.

This was already ridiculous, and I had a mile to go. I'd never seen flak like it. It came from a dozen posts, some of it bearing down on me from towers, anyone with a rifle—or Luger even —joining in. Bosquet was like a stirred up nest of blue ants, figures emerging from huts and buildings and hangars, all hell-bent on watching or contributing to my destruction.

It was the same old story: there was no stopping, no turning back, no escape. Whether I got a Victoria Cross or a 20 mm cannon shell on my chest, my fate was out of my hands. And from now on, halfway across the field, with the twin jet in my sights, evasion was absolutely out of the question.

Steady on the target, left hand down to camera switch. The jet's nose was dead center in my sight, tricycle undercarriage, the two black orifices of the turbos, the black muzzles of the formidable nose armament, the square-cut raised tailplane. It was all implanted upon my mind for all time, with the multicolored explosions of crossfire following me as close as a trailed streamer.

A hundred yards short of the plane I lifted my Tiffy fifty feet, sailed over the top at around 410 mph with a prayer uttered at twice that speed that they had not hit my camera.

A four-barrel 20 mm gun post was dead ahead, seven-man crew intent on only one thing. The tracers arched lazily towards me at first, then speeded up and became a multicolored torrent of high explosive.

I should have held my temper, just given my mind to evasion, with prayers to the Almighty that by some miracle I was still airborne. Instead, I pushed the stick forward, raised the center dot of my sight a fraction above the weapon and its crew, checked turn and bank for a steady line, and gave it a long five-second burst, all the way in.

It was two cannon against four. But I had the advantages of

a fixed target and an accumulation of vengeful adrenalin. I did not look back. I wanted no lip-smacking satisfaction at the death of others. And, as this thought flashed through my mind dazed by the speed and light and sound of battle, my engine stopped, just like that, without any preliminary hesitancy. So —retribution anyway. I had about thirty seconds to select a field, and put her down. And probably not much more than a minute after that to blow her up with portfires ready for this destruction on the left of my seat.

Fuel to off, no time to pump down flaps, arms crossed to grab handles and release doors simultaneously . . . The procedure was instinctive. Then suddenly not necessary. The engine gave an explosion like a field howitzer, thought better of quitting, decided the mocking joke was over, and roared back into life, seemingly fitter than ever.

I reckoned I was a mile southeast of Bosquet. They knew I would not return, not after surviving two miracles of crossfire. Their eyes would be on the 109s already airborne, and others no doubt panic-scrambling right now. So I decided to return, opened up to full throttle again, banked at 90 degrees around some farm buildings, made life hell for a herd of milked cows emerging from a barn.

It was easy now that I had my bearings. I could hug the land closer than ever, even having to lift up over low hedges, brushing my air intake on the tops of some saplings, and then was over the barbed-wire perimeter. Seen, briefly, from left to right, were water tanks, six domestic huts—probably airmen's living quarters—a raised flak post, parade ground, and beyond, the Heinkels flanking the jet.

I opened fire at 400 yards, shots falling low, scoring the ground, sending up flashes and puffs of gravel and earth. I did not stop firing, did not raise the sight—reduced range would deal with that. And began hitting. I hit for three seconds with my two cannon, some sixty high explosive and incendiary and armor-piercing shells. And I swear not one of them missed.

The jet must have already been a ruin when I pulled up over. But it was not until I climbed to 250 feet a mile or two later, pursued now by every flak gun in the vicinity, that I saw that it was on fire and that only tortured alloy and steel would be left for the Luftwaffe Development Section—TLR / FL-E.

CHAPTER ELEVEN

A Long Way Home

I had plotted a course home, memorized the landmarks, noted the red cross-hatched flak zones, checked where I should best come out over the coast. But as I suspected it might be, the simple act of swift escape was my only concern, and I simply set 355 degrees on the compass, noted the bearing of the sun on my right when on this course, and gave my concentration to flying unreasonably low without unreasonably putting an immediate end to my life by hitting something.

The town of Mamers was a gray smudge on my right, the sun's rays cutting through the industrial haze. A dead straight road coincided with my course and I saw cyclists ahead hastily dismounting, some to wave, others to throw themselves in the ditch. I lifted momentarily to give myself time to check wings and tailplane for flak damage but could find no more than the pepper holes in my port wing. The engine's roar was steady, the fuel situation not impossible—about twenty gallons left in main tanks. I kept the boost at +1, revs at just under 3,000, which gave 290 mph. Less would put me at a grave disadvantage if I were jumped, more would use up fuel too rapidly. And

I deleted from my mind, as I had deleted that jet prototype with my cannon, the undeniable fact that every fighter squadron in France would be after my blood, and every flak gunner at his post, fingers quivering over trigger.

Everything was fine, I told myself. Here was the Orne, a lovely lazy river flowing north between rich meadows, a few early morning fishermen on the banks, swearing roundly *"Ah, merde alors!"* as I swept past, wingtips almost level with their rods.

Let's be clear, I was not being slackly pleased with myself. I was too old a hand for that. I was aileroning to check the sky to right and left, and glancing in the mirror every few seconds. But at that precise time on this gem of a summer day, racing down this river with a set of pricelessly valuable photographs on board, and with the exhilaration of successful accomplishment, I was feeling very good.

At the same time, so certain was I that my luck could not be sustained at this ridiculously high peak for very much longer, it was almost with relief that I spotted directly above, at no more than 3,000 feet, a finger-formation *schwarm* of four F.W.190s. They were crossing right to left, no doubt one of many patrols airborne to intercept me between Le Mans and the coast. I ruddered rapidly away from the river, which would show me up too clearly, and watched them fade into the distance.

Somewhere near Argentan, still close to the river and skimming the topmost branches of a pine forest, I was picked up by an alert spotter on a flak tower. It spat 40 and 20 mm tracers at extreme range, very accurate as usual, and I jinked and climbed to give myself maneuvering room, and flinched a mile to the east. They did not touch me, though they were close, but now the word of my position and heading would be around.

Two *schwarms* of 109s picked me up within three minutes. They were Fs, not as fast as my Tiffy, but eight against one and every advantage on their side. I watched them break up into four pairs, the first pair—sleek and evil, flaunting their black crosses and swastikas—came in at 4 o'clock on my right side, the second pair already peeling off for a similar pass on my left.

Now my fuel consumption would soar! Wide open throttle. Ready to break. My intention was to turn into them, let them dissipate their diving speed advantage, and then use my superior speed to get clear. There were as many ifs as miles to the coast. But it was the only way.

The first 109's wing cannon sparkled at 500 yards. *Not* an experienced pilot, I decided. When the second opened fire at 300, I hauled back on the stick with both hands and kicked left rudder, almost stall-turned into the ground, saw the blue-gray splash of river below me, pushed down so low that my prop tips just grazed the water, banked steeply around an island thick with willow, climbed to get my bearings, and slammed through the gate for emergency boost. The sky above was clear. Then I spotted a single 109—God, how good their camouflage paint was!—lower than I was and right on his wing-tip against a background of trees. He was in the full momentum of his dive and flying faster than I was. To turn again would lose me speed and distance. Instead, I elevator-jinked, pumping the stick to and fro with all my strength, stressing the tailplane where the Tiffy was most vulnerable.

The tracers were like snow on a blizzard wind. I felt a thud in my port wing and had to force the stick hard right to hold her horizontal. But still pumping to throw off the pilot's aim. He was dead behind me, firing professionally in short bursts. A church ahead, tall spire again. I aileroned and kicked my way around it, glimpsed a cobbled square filled with people, horses rearing.

I couldn't last. I knew it. Too lucky until now for it to hold out. All right, no pictures, but no prototype either. At least I had got the devil, and—boy!—would they miss her. . . .

The fire from the rear had stopped. A glance in the mirror revealed nothing. My A.S.I. showing 425 mph. They really had boosted this engine. And with a port wing torn open to knock 20 mph off the speed. My right arm was going to feel the strain. I eased back the throttle, checked the fuel gauge below the rev counter, noted nil on main tanks, and turned the control lever on the right of the cockpit to nose tanks.

A squadron of Focke-Wulfs harassed me next, coming in from the east, out of the sun, turning for a beam attack, closing in very fast, faster than the 109s—stubby-evil rather than sleek-evil. There was nothing I could do but repeat my tactics of turning in and recovering my course as fast as possible—all at emergency boost, the 100-octane fuel pouring through my carburetors like Niagara, so that, if they did' not knock me down here, I would be ditching in mid-Channel.

Weary of daisy-cutting and the concentration it demanded, I suddenly pulled back the stick and climbed flat out, leaving the 109s behind but exposing myself to heavy flak and to anything else higher than I was. But now I could also see the coast ahead, giving me a surge of hope: the great dark spread of Le Havre, the wide estuary of the Seine, and now—almost below me—Trouville, Deauville, playgrounds of rich gamblers until the war, now heavy with gun emplacements and minefields.

The heavy flak peppered the sky to right and left, above and below, but mostly behind, thank God, my exceptional speed confusing their aim. One heavy shell was close enough to rock me almost on to my back, and again I caught the cordite scent like a puff of death in the cockpit. My Tiffy survived, though my right arm was feeling the strain of compensating for that torn wing.

When the flak suddenly ceased, I knew worse was to come. They were clearing the air for the fighters yet again. I was at 6,000 now, right over the coast, the sun hot from my right; and 5,000 above, Razor Eyes saw them all right and wished he had not. Best not to read the preface to your own funeral. Twelve,

eighteen, twenty-four. My God, they had put up the whole
Luftwaffe for me.

The first squadron was peeling off, one, two, three, in turn,
like dive bombers. I waited for them to come, with nothing to
do except put my nose gently down for yet more speed, poised
ready to kick my way from death. But then there would be
another, and another. . . .

"Tallyho, chaps!" It was a lovely, fruity voice, as English
and rich as scones with Cornish cream. "Nine o'clock below.
Going down now."

Not a sound had come from my earphones since leaving
England except the crackle of static. But this voice was absurdly close as well as absurdly English, and I strained my eyes
looking into the sun, and then spotted the twinkle of fighters,
the graceful curved full wings of Spitfires—Bruno's beloved
Spitfires—at 20,000 feet or higher, a whole wing of these angels
of relief and mercy. And they were coming down.

Another deeper voice: "Barstow Leader, I think that's our
Tiffy at 10 o'clock, about angels five, I'd guess."

"Yes, that's me," I wanted to shout. "Come on—not much
time."

Instead, I tried to keep my voice steady. "Barstow Leader,
this is Juno. I am right below you and short of fuel."

Then I had to pull hard into a climbing turn to evade the
first of the 109s. The Spitfires were all around me by the time
I had recovered. They were Mark IXs, equal to the Messerschmitts if not as fast as the Focke-Wulfs. Performance com-
parisons were irrelevant as far as I was concerned. I hated to
leave this scrap—and what a scrap it was going to be—but
home called.

I dived almost vertically for the sea, leveled off above the
wavetops, looked back to see nothing, absolutely nothing behind or above. And checked my fuel.

It was worse than I had feared. Thirty gallons in the nose
tanks. Enough to get me three-quarters of the way across the
Channel at full weak mixture, coarse pitch, 2,300 rpm, + 1¾

boost. Halfway across if I had any more fighting to do. Oh well, it was a good try! Just too much opposition.

I climbed very gently, preferring to bail out to ditching. A pair of Spitfires had been detached to escort me, one on either side, canopies slid back, the pilots raising a thumb in turn as I nodded towards them. No point in breaking radio silence. Better to leave the enemy in doubt about my fate.

The engine rumbled on. I pretended I could see the faint smudge of the English coast, but of course it was still far beyond visibility. I thought of Bruno again, imagined him in one of the escorting Spits, canopy thrown back, grinning across at me.

I thought, "If only to God I could get at that camera, extract the film, wrap it in waterproof." I thought, "If only those Spits would close in, and when my engine gives up, each lend me a wing." Then I knew my mind was wandering after the long strain, and I wound open my right window to let in air.

I could see it now. It *was* the coast all right. On this clear morning, the white cliffs of the Isle of Wight to the left, the white cliffs beyond Brighton to the right. And at the same moment, the engine began to spit, and at once expired, leaving me in an unnatural silence. The Tiffy's nose dropped like a head for the executioner's block, and one of the Spitfire pilots began transmitting "Mayday."

I had been at 5,000, and was already at 4,000. The drill for bailing out was to seize the door jettison levers, right hand to left door and vice versa, for extra purchase, and pull hard simultaneously. Then detach R / T plug and oxygen tube clip, release straps, push the stick forward hard. And out you went. Theoretically. Hoping not to strike the tail which would either kill you or knock you out with the result that you failed to pull the ripcord. Simple, they had said.

I remembered it all. I remembered something else, too. There *could* be a drain left in the main tanks. Impossible, but —just a drain?

So I switched the cock over to main again. Nothing happened, and I was down to 2,500, the sea uncomfortably close. A shudder. An explosion, silence. Then another explosion— and like the triumphal chorus at the climax of Handel's *Messiah*, the Sabre restarted in full song.

The reaction was interesting. I began to fly again, as if nothing had happened. The Spitfire on my right, which had remained in loose formation, tucked in closer. The second Spitfire suddenly dived, pulled up, and did a perfect, graceful, celebratory slow roll. Then resumed station.

I was about two miles from the coast when the engine died again. I immediately selected flaps and undercart down in the hope that there might be enough hydraulic power left to assist. Whatever else happened now, a crushing belly wheels-up landing with this precious camera and film in the fuselage was out of the question. There was no response. The Tiffy was a flying corpse that would not fly for long. Not long enough to reach land. Or would she? I put the propeller into full coarse pitch, kept her nose up until the speed fell to just under 150 A.S.I., stretching the glide to the maximum, and noting with gratitude that the wind had backed south.

Like most Tiffy pilots, I had developed the habit of keeping one eye open for fields large enough for an emergency landing. But this landing had to be wheels down, requiring a long unbroken stretch. And there was nothing in sight beyond the coast road except gardens and commercial greenhouses, even if my glide would take me that far.

Then I saw that the tide was out, folding waves leaving a narrow strip of sand separating the sea from the banked pebble higher up. I still had a thousand feet and might just make it to this sand strip.

Speed down to 120, too close to a stall. I put the nose down fractionally, again selected full flaps and undercart down, seized the emergency hydraulics pump with my left hand and thrust it to and fro, felt the yaw as the wheels locked home and noted the three green lights on the dash with relief. Then turned through 90 degrees parallel with the shore, released the doors with a violent double pull, and the wind tore into the cockpit.

The Tiffy crabbed in on the crosswind at ninety, and I aimed for the narrow strip of sand clear of the breakwaters, still shining wet in the early morning sun, with the waves washing lightly over it, held her off, and dropped the heavy machine from ten feet.

She did not go over on to her nose at once, which was ladylike of her, and contrary to the rules of balance. She bounced, sending up a sheet of spray, ran for 300 yards almost out of control. Then the right wheel caught the end of one of the breakwaters and she reared up on to her nose, throwing me hard against my straps.

The silence was broken by the sound of dripping oil, the creaking of suddenly cooled metal, and the voice of Bruno from the distant past: "*Not* a perfect three-pointer!"

Later, some troops from a nearby battery helped me out. It was a long business because they first had to cut their way through the barbed-wire defense that ran along the top of the beach, and use a mine detector before they could reach me. By this time, I had used the emergency tool kit to extract the big black camera from its belly housing, and was clutching it like a baby, with the rising tide around my knees.

"What's that you've got there, sir?" the corporal in charge asked.

"Just some seaside snaps," I said, trying to laugh, and wondering how I could be shaking so much in this hot summer sun.

After a mug of army tea I told the corporal I needed one of his trucks. I drove it myself, feeling more comfortable with something to do, taking a special satisfaction in driving fast and safely while my subconscious kept hammering away: "You're alive, you pushed your luck and it held!"

Back at Ford, Spurling took the camera from me. It was only a few hours since we had met, and now I felt I had known him all my life. "So the stately goddess, Juno, made it."

"With about a yard to spare," I said. He thought I was

joking, and said, "Good show. And now let's look at your pretty pictures."

Unlike that first dice with the 109, the camera had not failed me. In spite of the speed and all that hot metal whistling around me, there were a dozen shots of the jet, showing every detail.

"Better the devil you know," said Spurling slowly as he held them up. "These'll interest the boffins."

CHAPTER TWELVE

"Quite Time!"

My mother said, "We'll go in here," and pushed open the restaurant door. "What do you mean you don't deserve it? Of course you deserve it." She sat down at a table before the head waiter could get near us. "So stop this silly talk, Mick."

Jo said, "She's right, Mick. Of course you deserved a gong." Jo had been out of the hospital for a month now, convalescing at home, looking pale but much steadier, and very changed. No sign of the old competition and provocation of our childhood; instead, the gentle benevolence of someone who has been through the fire, as she had.

Bruno's mother and father, used to my mother's ways, sat down as they were ordered, and Bruno's mother said, "Bruno carried on just the same when he got his D.F.C. too. I can't understand why you all carry on like that."

Vivienne and Bruno's parents had come to Buckingham Palace with my mother and father and Jo for the investiture. I had hated the whole business, knowing I deserved nothing, knowing that only fate had guided me into the R.A.F. in the first place, had then steered me into Fighter Command, and even on to this last show which had earned me an immediate D.F.C.

And God, and holy luck, and the chance of fate again, had caused me to survive and be sitting down here, with my mother ordering for everyone. It was nothing to do with the stunning fear which had once hit me, nothing to do with courage, any of this, I now knew. Nothing deserving special praise or gongs. I was no more than a small cog in the war machine system, more complex even than a Tiffy's engine, my pace conforming with the opening and closing of the throttle. Conformity, that was what it was all about. You conformed to what was expected of you, to the system, to the machine's need, and to the forces of fate. That day, if we had been on Striding Edge, I suppose I would have recovered that ruck-sack. Not because I was more or less brave (whatever that means) but because I had learned to do what was expected of me. That's all.

Vivienne clutched my hand supportingly under the table, and my father managed to get a word in edgeways: "Didn't he look nice—the King, I mean? Dignified and grand but human, too."

"Of course he's human," my mother said. Then she ad-dressed herself to Vivienne and asked crisply, indicating me with a nod of her head, "When's he going to ask you to marry him? Quite time."

I did later in the day, with both of us giggling, and Vivienne said, "Message received and understood. I'll think it over—over, over."

She did say "Yes." Otherwise, forty-one years later, we would not have just moved together (which, of course, is why I found Bruno's old letter in the first place) to Dunedin in South Island, New Zealand, having farmed near Milton ever since the end of the war. And otherwise we would not have had five children, all grown up now, with children of their own—all with razor-sharp eyes and none of them with experience of war, thank the Lord.

Glossary of Terms and Abbreviations

aileroning   maneuvering plane by operating the ailerons

Aldis lamp   a signaling lamp

angels five   code word for five thousand feet

A.S.I.   Air Speed Indicator

A.T.A.   Air Transport Auxiliary

balloons   large numbers of balloons secured by cables as a defense against low-flying enemy planes

blast pen   parking place for planes protected from bomb blast by earth or sandbags

boffins   slang for scientists

bought it   got killed

brolley hop   escape by parachute

chopped   killed: thus chop rate, or number of fatal casualties

circus   a large concentration of aircraft

C.O.   Commanding Officer

cone, coning   a concentration of antiaircraft fire, or flak, at one point in the sky contrail   white vapor created by planes flying at height under certain climatic conditions

deflection   the angle of fire required to hit a fast-moving target. Thus half ring deflection, or a maneuver of a fighter plane with fixed forward facing guns aimed with a reflected ring and center dot on the windshield.

D.F.C.   Distinguished Flying Cross

D.F.M.   Distinguished Flying Medal

dice   a fight

dispersal   a collection of small buildings scattered about an airfield to minimize bomb damage

dodgy   risky

donny   a fight involving many planes

E.F.T.S.   Elementary Flying Training School

elevator-jink   jerking a plane rapidly up and down by pushing the control column backwards and forwards rapidly in order to confuse an enemy's aim

erks   low-rank ground crew who service planes

flak   German antiaircraft fire

flamer   a plane that crashes on fire, much dreaded by pilots

fuel bowser   a tanker truck for refueling planes

gen   information, derived from Intelligence

go for a Burton   be killed

gong   a medal

Gosport tube   a flexible tube with earphones and mouthpiece, for communication between an instructor and a pupil pilot

half ring deflection   *see* deflection

intruder   a fighter that searches for enemy planes in the dark close to their airfields where they are especially vulnerable taking off and landing

I.O.   Intelligence Officer

Irvine jacket   a fur-lined leather flying jacket

jerry   a German or a German plane

jink   *see* elevator-jink

kite   slang for airplane

M.C.   Military Cross, a medal

met.   meteorological, or weather, information

N.A.A.F.I.   Navy, Army, and Air Force Institutes

N.C.O.   Noncommissioned Officer

Nissen hut   a small steel hut

op(s)   operation: action against the enemy, also a ground unit controlling ops

O.T.U.   Operational Training Unit, the final stage of training

pitot head   a hollow tube in the wing that measures pressures, and thus airspeed

P.R.U.   Photographic Reconnaissance Unit

R.A.F.V.R.   Royal Air Force Volunteer Reserve

ramrod   an offensive operation

rate-two turn   Rate refers to steepness of turn, recorded on an instrument. Rate two is moderately steep.

R.D.F.   Radio Direction Finding, code cover for early radar

revs   speed in revolutions of engine's crankshaft

rhubarb   a single plane sortie, usually at low level

ring (on sleeve)   a mark of rank

rpm   revolutions per minute

R / T   Radio Telephone

scramble   a rushed takeoff to meet the enemy

sector recce   reconnaisance of the area for which an airfield or airfields is responsible

Sidcot suit   a one-piece zipped-up flying suit

sprog   a beginner

sweep   a large-scale offensive flight over enemy territory to provoke action

tip and run   a rapid surprise raid at low level

trolley acc   a small wheeled device to carry batteries for starting a plane's engine

troops   *see* erks

Very (signal)   a shell fired from a large bore pistol giving off a bright light, usually as a warning

V.H.F.   Very High Frequency (referring to radio)

W.A.A.F.   Women's Auxiliary Air Force

About the Author

Richard Hough says, "*Razor Eyes* stems from my experiences forty years ago, except that I was trained in southern California. But I flew Hurricanes and Typhoons in combat and felt much as the main character about the early days of doubt. I also had exceptional eyesight.

"This is in no way an autobiographical story, but facts and feelings are still close in my memory. The idea had been milling about for some time, and in a curious way I think my recall after this stretch of time has more veracity and objectivity than if I had put this down years ago."

Mr. Hough is the author of numerous novels, travel books, and biographies, including *Mountbatten.* Several of his books have appeared in the *New Yorker* magazine. He has been writing children's books for many years under the pseudonym Bruce Carter. *Razor Eyes* is his first novel for young adults to be published under his real name.

Richard Hough lives in Gloucestershire, England.